Embraced

Written and illustrated by

Blaine Turner

The Dollhouse Trilogy

Book 1 - **Trapped**
Book 2 - **Captive**
Book 3 - **Embraced**

Embraced

Copyright © 2008

by

Blaine P. Turner

All rights reserved

ISBN 978-0-578-00497-6

This is a work of fiction. Names, characters, places, and incidents either are the product of the author's imagination or are used fictitiously, and any resemblance to actual persons, living or dead, business establishments, events, or locales is entirely coincidental.

This little book is dedicated with love to
my daughter Krista

~1~
Queen of Beasts

First of all if you haven't finished the books <u>Trapped</u> and <u>Captive</u> then silly you. Go back and complete them. Okay, if you don't *have* them, that's fine. You can still read this book, but if you don't understand everything, it's not my fault. Come to think of it, you've probably heard all this before, so just sit back and relax, I'll get right to the story.

Mary is a nice young girl about your age, if you are twelve that is, who lived with an elderly woman she called "Aunt Clara." She called her that because that's what all us kids called her, even after she died. Even after we were all grown up. I don't think she was really Mary's aunt, but I'm still figuring that out. I'll be sure to let you know when I do, hopefully before the end of this book.

My name is William and I come into the story later. I'm not a kid anymore, otherwise how could I be writing a real book like this? Some of you may already know me. I've grown quite handsome, with a beard and an important job in a local restaurant. You know your job is important when the company gives you lots of keys and a cell phone. Unfortunately they don't also give you a wife. That, you have to look for yourself, and on my salary, well – sad news. I do have a cat though, a quite reasonable substitute. But more about me later. I suppose you're presuming this story has something to do with a girl.

Well, you're right. It's Mary. Mary, the one with the long, flowing brown hair, striking green eyes, and a wonderful smile. She was well mannered and accomplished in all sorts of girl talents such as cooking, sewing and singing. She made everything she wore look good. And she was *nice*. Why she was even nice to the bugs in Aunt Clara's garden. They were her friends. Was she sheltered? Oh my yes. Innocent? To the extreme. Naïve? To the max. But feisty? Overly so. Twelve going on sixteen, you might say, and just bursting to get out into the big world of malls, movies and you guessed it, men. Well, boys at least.

But her Aunt Clara is a bit odd. So is her house. Strange. Like no TV, no magazines. Picture it. And no going out either. Only straight into and out of church, which was boring to her. No staring at the other kids either because there is something wrong with them. All of them. Of course, after a while Mary figured out that there was nothing wrong with them at all. It must have been her that was unusual.

People always looked at her in funny ways, as if they couldn't take their eyes off her for some reason.

"Oh, Mary my dear," Aunt Clara would always say, "you are so special. Never mind if people stare. Life is not a beauty pageant you know. So don't fret about yourself. Just hold your head up if you can. God loves you just as you are. And inner beauty is what counts in His book. And I love you too, of course.

"And dinner is ready. Wake up Mary. Dinner is ready."

Dinner indeed was ready. As usual, the table was long and fancy. The food was steaming in bowls, as tiny drops of water formed on the outsides of stemmed glassware. The tablecloth was lace, as was Mary's pretty dress. Everything appeared warm and cozy in the candlelight. But Mary's eyes were moist because deep within her she kept an awful secret. You see, she believed what everyone else must know by just looking – that she was not really beautiful on the outside. But her burden and indeed her tragedy was how ugly she viewed herself on the *inside* as well.

Ugly. So she thought. So she was led to believe. But you know her, don't you? What do *you* think?

Mary's dinner was pleasant and plentiful, as usual, but there was only Aunt Clara to share it with. Always only Aunt Clara. Forever only boring Aunt Clara. Finally Mary decided to do something about it. Knowing full well the real dangers on the third floor, she decided to explore instead the dark and dusty basement which housed only a barrel of apples, some rusty tools, and... Who knows? Maybe she'd dig up some luscious, dark secret down there. A skeleton perhaps. A hidden diary. An old pistol. If not, she could always dream up some pretend danger that would bring mouth-watering horror to even her most tedious days.

And nights. That's when she planned go down there. In the dead of night. Right among the dark and decaying basement things. There had to be ghouls and surely a fiend. This fiend would be enticingly wicked, tantalizingly naughty, temptingly masculine. But in her imagination she'd be more than a match for that. She'd meet him head-on in hand-to-hand combat. Even toe-to-toe, if he dared. He'd try to frighten her by making faces and rude gestures, but being a twelve year old girl, she was more than expert at that. So she thought anyway. Do you think she was not capable of reaching down a hidden and forbidden book or two from Aunt Clara's top shelf? Do you think she didn't make any discoveries in them?

So the fiend would try to stare her down, but her eyes would consume his. He'd try to hurl insults at her, but she'd made up some mighty nasty words herself and how to deliver them with withering effect. Finally in desperation, he'd pick her up bodily and carry her off. Back in his lair would ensue the fight of their lives. A desperate, delicious battle, lasting for days. For you see, what monster has a corner on ugliness? What man-beast has not met his match? For isn't the startling repulsiveness of a deformed female child so much more unbearable than the expected grossness of an adult male, however monstrous? Her weapons were the more powerful, her resolve the more overwhelming. In this case the beast would ultimately succumb and become hers to command, Along with all his buddies, of course. "Master of all monsters," she whispered and her insides tightened. "Queen of beasts," she breathed out loud, and raised a fist in the air.

The wind blew a curtain open and startled her. So how bad could it be? She pulled her fist out of the air and crawled safely into bed. She waited till well past midnight. Then, robed in her flowing, flannel nightgown, she swept down and stood at last before the basement door. Swallowing hard, she timidly touched the old brass knob and slowly it became cold to her fingers. She turned it slightly, but it squealed and fought back. Her hand sprung off it, but she put it right back and turned harder. Again the knob complained, but soon ceased struggling and its bolt popped free from the striker plate. Click, groan, creak.

Now the rusty door hinges were rasping and sending chills up and down her spine. As they opened, a cold, musty smell engulfed her from the slit of darkness. She felt like sneezing but with superhuman effort was able to control it, for she had read somewhere that to sneeze is to lose your soul for a period of time. She would need her soul down there in the basement, and every ounce of her courage as well.

"Oh those poor basement-dwelling creatures," she made herself believe. "When they gaze on my hideous face they will vomit and flee in utter terror. Then I will be free to fight the monster who would steal my heart. Instead, I will capture his."

Her real heart pounded faster and faster as she descended the old, protesting stairs and placed her tiny white feet on the cold cement floor. Glancing about defensively, at first she saw only apples. Big dusty bushel baskets of them. Then whole barrels filled to the brim with them. Where all these apples could have come from, she hadn't a clue, but they were there nevertheless. She was tempted to bite into one but even in the dim light, they looked dusty, and well, she had to admit, possibly more than a little poisonous.

"All apples in fairy tales are poisonous," she said to herself. "At least the scary ones like this."

"This isn't that scary," intruded a voice close to her shoulder.

She turned immediately and gazed into the mud-stained face of a boy scarcely an inch taller than herself. Yes, a boy. Actually he looked more like an escaped convict. He wore a dirty, striped t-shirt and there was blood mixed with gravel across his arm. Yet his voice was surprisingly deep for a boy, especially one with such big adorable eyes, and his manner was entirely too bold for a mere youth.

Mary was quite sure she was dreaming. She just blinked hard at him once or twice.

Then he said, "Don't scream, dream girl. I'm only looking for a place to hole up for a day or two. Then I'll return to my real foster home. I live far, far away. Will you hide me?"

Hide him? Oh my goodness, she wanted to keep him forever. But Mary had never spoken to a real boy alone before. Certainly she had traded sweet nothings with many imaginary ones. Yet none quite so fetching as this real one. So she lowered her eyes, nervously combed her hair with her fingers and said:

"Wee-oh-goo." What came out was a cross between a burp and a belch. Putting her hand to her mouth, she headed, mortified toward the stairs. Half way up a hand grabbed the hem of her nightgown and held tight.

"Can you at least bring me some food?" he pleaded.

"Sh-sure," she choked, glancing down into his tangled black hair, "will you eat a chicken leg?"

"Sh-sure," he answered with a wry smile, "any part will do." With his eyes, he seemed to add, "And you're the loveliest creature I've ever set my gaze upon. I could eat you up as well."

Her knees buckled and she almost fell down the steps – but recovered and stared into his face. Their eyes met and held.

"Incredible," she thought, "either he's blind, an idiot, or I'm not as ugly as I was led to believe."

"Are you going to let go of my nightgown?" she said out loud.

With some effort he did just that and she disappeared upstairs. Ten minutes later she returned with a drumstick neatly wrapped in a fancy, paper napkin and tied with a nice ribbon. Her hair was combed and there was a dab of powder on her nose. She smelled of too much perfume. But he was gone. In fact there was no evidence that he had ever been there.

Tossing the chicken aside, she gazed around the basement with watery eyes. "I'll hide you in my heart, young prince," she sighed. But he was gone. Instead of a monster, she had met a man. A man who had never been there, but who nevertheless had thought she was beautiful.

"It only takes one," she reflected as she pulled the blankets aside and once again began tucking herself into bed. Then she noticed an unmistakable smear of mud on the hem of her nightgown. Unmistakable, at least to her, and that's all that counts. Tenderly, she pulled it under the blankets with her.

~2~
Running Away

Mary's heart was so stirred by the incident with the boy, real or not, that she decided to run away and find her very own prince-apparent. To do this she had two choices – flee out into the real world, with its real dangers and real unknowns – or return to the magic mansion she had come from. In the mansion at least she would have friends and familiar surroundings. Not to mention fun and all the free junk food a girl could eat. Quite frankly she was fed up with Aunt Clara's wholegrain bread, corn-fed beef and organic vegetables. And she was growing painfully sick and fat with her jellyrolls and pies.

It took her three nights to put her plan into action. On night one, in a moment of weakness, instead of heading up to the third floor, she went back down into the basement. In her hand she carried a pathetic looking peanut butter and jelly sandwich. In her heart she carried a pathetic longing for someone to give it to. She saw only a rat. Not an intelligent, talking one like up on the third floor, but a dumb, disgusting barn rat with no redeeming qualities whatsoever. Certainly it would take her sandwich, she thought, but never her heart. Not seeing any male idols, men, or even boys to give it to, she left the sandwich on the workbench and hoped the rat would gag on the sticky peanut butter.

As she was climbing the stairs she spied something on one of the steps halfway up. Bending down, she retrieved a chicken bone with a bow neatly tied around its middle. "Impossible!" She recoiled. She glanced back into the blackness, but it was pointless. Of course, he was just toying with her. Playing with her emotions. She tossed the bone over by the P, B and J. and slammed the door on her way out. She was upset, so she went straight to bed. No tears, no fond wishes or dreams. Just the safe retreat of sleep.

On the next night she made doubly sure that Aunt Clara was fast asleep, then went to retrieve the big key from the roll top desk. There it was, bigger and more beat-up than all the others. But it had more character and history than all the others combined. Oh the secrets it could unlock. I'd be ashamed to write them here. Well, I guess I'm writing one of them right now, aren't I? So, yes, Mary stole the key, stole up the stairs and silently unlocked the door to the third floor. Then she retreated back down the two flights of stairs and buried the key safely back in its exact spot in the roll-top drawer. By this time it was late and Mary was so tired, or was it afraid, that again she just went back to bed. This time, however, her thoughts and dreams were of seeing her friends in the enchanted mansion once more.

On the third night she tiptoed all the way up to stand timidly before the tiny, but impressive Mousumerset Manor. Everything seemed the same as when she had left. As when I had freed her from being trapped in it, that is. And got locked in myself for my troubles. But you've already read that story. The great house still had four stories, and eight tall chimneys. On top it still had a guard railed widow's walk and a tall ship weathervane.

The heavy, miniature drapes were still at the windows and the beds were still made with thin little sheets. Mary noticed the linens on her bed had been changed and there was no water in the miniature basin or pitcher on her washstand. The mice had always made sure she had fresh water. Still, there were dozens of bottles of bubble bath to be seen. Every sort and kind. Oh how she longed to make use of one right then.

She knelt down and called out the name, "Luucy." She had forgotten, of course, that voice sounds don't travel into the house. "Ivanhoho," she tried again, but to no avail. So she decided to just walk in the front door.

Silly her. She also forgot that adults, and even big kids couldn't just go in or out at will. That was the enchantment. Well that was a bummer. Now her plans were dashed. She would have to go all the way downstairs and out the front door, to try running away in the real world. But it was the dead of night and probably chilly outside. And she had no money, no credit card, no friends, no nothing! Not even a flashlight.

Just then a small insect came to her rescue. Actually it was a tiny, delicate mayfly. Mary looked sideways at it and pretended she didn't notice. It was annoying. It kept buzzing about her in the semidarkness. So Mary finally addressed it.

"Okay Mayrie, I apologize for treating you so horribly in the last book, okay. I was having a bad night. I'm sorry I called you a moth."

The mayfly just sat there staring at her.

"Okay Mayrie, you're not carrying a grudge are you? I said I was sorry. What more do you want?"

The mayfly just sat there staring at her.

"Okay, if you want to be that way, why don't you just buzz off."

"I wish to help you," it said.

"Even after what I did to you?" replied Mary.

"I've never met you before," said the mayfly.

"What? You're Mayrie, aren't you?" hissed Mary.

"Sure, but I'm Mayrie the 653rd. I think you knew Mayrie the 485th, who was actually a lacewing fly. We look quite similar. She died of a broken heart, you know."

"I don't want to talk about it," said Mary.

"But I wish to help you," repeated the mayfly.

"What. To be a better person? To not be ugly? Is that what you're saying?" snapped Mary.

"I just wish to help you," said the mayfly, burying her head in two of her six hands. "I think I'm feeling ill."

Mary began to feel sorry for it. "Okay, how do you want to help me?"

"I can get you into the mansion."

"Really? How?"

"By telling you my story."

"How will that help?"

"Please, do you want to hear my story? I don't have much time and I'm feeling ill."

"Okay, okay," said Mary, rolling her eyes, "tell away, if it will make you happy."

The mayfly immediately began sobbing, but then started talking through her tears. "I was born into the light of day only this morning. And such a beautiful dawn it was, after so many months in the muck at the bottom of the goldfish pond out there. I quickly dried out and tried my wings on a wisp of wind. Such a feeling, I must tell you, to be able to soar above the trees and then dive at will through El's great green pastures. I did it time and again, just for the pure joy of it. I felt so free and fabulous, playing tag with the leaves, and peek-a-boo with the sun.

"Then just when everything was simply wonderful, it all got even better. I met a man. I mean a mayfly-man. He was everything a girl could dream of. Distinguished, dashing, dangerous. Entirely a dude. And fresh, well you don't know the half of it. He held my hand and even kissed me on the mouthparts. But then he was gone in a flash and I never even caught his name. You'd think he'd at least give me his name, wouldn't you? Or want to know mine. But insects are that way, I suppose. We don't know any better.

"Anyway, I considered myself married, after a fashion, so I settled lightly upon the pond of my birth and laid my eggs. I can't say that this was the most thrilling part of my existence so far, but it was somehow satisfying to be fulfilling El's driving purpose for my life. To lay eggs.

"Now all this has happened before two o'clock this afternoon. So I thought about what to do next. Finding a better man was way up on my list, but I had a sneaking suspicion that I would find most of them disappointingly similar. So I decided to just glide and tumble through the marvelous garden all around me. Oh, I must tell you it was pure peace and joy. As lighthearted as a breeze, as carefree as a brook, that was me.

14

"Then from the top of a tree I spotted one of my mayfly-girlfriends upside-down on the grass below. Naturally I flew down to investigate but all I learned were her dying words, "We only live one day!"

~3~
The Mayfly Dies

"**O**ne day! We only live one day?" Mayrie continued her story. "My friend had to be lying. But there she was lying dead. What about all my hopes, dreams and aspirations? What about my plans for a new man, for college, for a cottage on a lake? Oh no. Just one day! And it was already five o'clock. I fell to the ground, feeling ill."

"You look okay now," interrupted Mary.

"Oh I'm not, I'm *not*," said the mayfly. "In fact, I'm so far gone that just a few minutes ago a bat refused to eat me. He said I looked stale. Imagine that, a picky bat! Then he told me a secret."

"You mean he talked," said Mary, "what was his name?"

"Ho hum," I think. No wait, it was "ho *ho*."

"You mean "Ivanhoho?" exclaimed Mary. "What did he tell you?"

"He said it was a secret."

"Did he tell you who it was a secret *from*?" demanded Mary, squinting her eyes.

"Well no."

"Aha, you see. Then you can tell me."

"Well, he said that if someone goes into that big house there, and then goes into another big house *inside* the big house, then they can become young again."

"That's true," said Mary "I've done it. Never mind, it's a long story. Why don't you do that instead of dying."

"Yes, that would be delightful, but the bat said I must die to self. I figure that means stop being selfish. So there's something written in the Harmony Code that says if someone dies for someone else, then they get to make a dying wish for that person, and it will come true."

"I never read that," said Mary blankly.

"Someone said it's in a footnote. Don't you read the footnotes? Anyway, it's my dying wish that you'd be able to enter Mousumerset Manor as soon as I breathe my last."

"Why would you do this for me?' asked Mary.

"Time is short and you are handy, my dear," said Mayrie, coughing hard and jerking her wings all out of kilter. "I'm a goner anyway, you might as well have something nice you want."

A small tear started down Mary's cheek but she wiped it away quickly so the dying mayfly wouldn't see it.

"But I don't want you to die," said Mary, here have a nice little bite from my candy bar."

This only made the mayfly sob and cough even harder, throwing her wings even more askew, and finally throwing her on her back in a heap. Dead. It was then that Mary saw that the mayfly didn't even have any mouthparts big enough to eat food. Hardly necessary if you only live one day, she fathomed. How awful of El to dream up such a creature! She tenderly picked up the limp body and placed it in the palm of her hand. Then she just sobbed and sobbed over it. How awful of El. How utterly awful of El.

Eventually she remembered the Harmony Code and poor Mayrie's dying wish. So gently enfolding the lifeless mayfly in her fingers, she tried the front door of Mousumerset Manor. It opened instantly and she popped in easily as – well, as a camel going through the eye of a needle. Seems impossible, but she had learned over and over again that with El, all things are possible.

Except one thing was different. As you know, insects don't shrink like people do when entering the manor. So the motionless body of the mayfly was suddenly huge in Mary's hand. Huge would be an understatement. It was like she was cradling some gigantic baby in her arms. Her baby. But a dead baby. How awful of El.

But then the baby stirred. Not only stirred, but blinked, yawned and smiled up into Mary's wide-eyed face. "My how you've shrunk," it said. "I suppose I've never seen all of your face before. It's very beautiful."

Mary's hands trembled with joy and she hugged the mayfly so hard she bent its wings out of shape. But it didn't seem to matter at all. Mayrie was just happy to be alive. And surprised too. They immediately made their way down the dark halls, up the dark staircases, and through the dark secret passageways – to the mysterious chambers of the bat Ivanhoho himself. Mary was always a bit timid around him because of his lofty language and highfalutin ideas and ideals – none of which she ever quite understood. But they were in luck, it was night and the bat was out. So they scurried straight into the old French Château which was standing invitingly in the corner.

~4~
Château Résurrection

The entrance foyer of the French Château seemed large as an entire house and the chairs along the wall were ornate and inviting, but much too fragile-looking to sit on. Mary and Mayrie just stood around trying not to break anything.

In due time a very rotund, red ladybug appeared. Before she had even crossed the wide hall Mayrie blurted out to her, "I just died to self, but rose again!"

The ladybug replied, "Good for you, Rosy. Welcome then to Château Résurrection. Here you can live forever. By the way, I was eavesdropping. The bat really said and I quote, 'If you die to self – if you lose your life – then you will gain it,' unquote. I suppose you didn't hear that last bit. Quite important. It's not your fault that you have such a short attention span. Of course the bat rarely makes any sense really, but this case appears to be an exception. I personally think he was talking about always getting your own way, rather than actually keeling over dead."

Here Mary flung herself over Marta almost killing the mayfly again in the process. Now embracing a giant ladybug is about as satisfying as hugging a garbage can, but Mary was simply glad to see her old friend.

"Marta," she said, "you've lost your funny accent."

"It's not funny," said Marta "You mean my lack-scent? I've been taking opera lessons and they say we have to learn to talk properly before we can learn to sing even one note. Even a flat one. I'm going to be a leading ladybug someday. A person of note. Many notes actually. But we have to wear lots of perfume like a stinkbug and low-rider necklines too. Why ever for, I'll never know. It *does* show all my legs off to good advantage, though. Very important for a full-figured soprano like myself. So what are you two in here for?"

"Never mind. I can guess," the ladybug went on without waiting for an answer. "For you Mayrie the 653rd there's a vacant princess' room way up in the central tower. Now get your abdomen on up there before midnight or you die for real. There's a headman, a footman and a muscleman up there to show you the way. Try the bubble bath, it might help some." With this, and without further ado she shooed the mayfly out the door. Mary had but a moment for a 'thank you' glance before her grace was on her way up to her new royal chambers.

"Now for you, Toodles," said the ladybug, "why are you back and what happened to your water boatman?"

"Oh, you mean Sir James? He became a real boy again, thank goodness," said Mary.

"And let me guess, you're back for a real man this time," said Marta.

"Well not really…"

"Of course you are. Be honest. Aren't we all?" puffed Marta.

Mary blushed and muttered, "I'm looking for my prince-apparent."

"Well, apparently I've got good news for you," said Marta. "We're well stocked with them right now. It's a buyer's market. Do you want a man complete with horse or without one?"

"Horse? No horse, thank you. I want to be the only love of his life."

"Well that narrows things down considerably," said Marta. "All real men have horses, or at least cars. In fact, there are only seven rooms upstairs with non-horse men in them, but only three are nonsmoking rooms as well. You don't look addicted to anything, so let's see, here are the keys to rooms 108, 214, and 401. The place is kind of a resort for men. Princes-apparent, I mean. Mind you, 401 is a loft in the attic. I'd only go there as a last resort."

"But I have one question, if I may," said Mary. "Are there human men in these rooms or are they only bugs pretending to be people?"

"Most men are bugs pretending to be people," replied the ladybug. "What do you expect in such a small book, Prince Charming? But they're all very male and searching for the women of their dreams. Don't be too picky here, Dearie. You can't afford it. They're very exciting and from all walks of life and running hot and cold in all fabrics and sizes from S to XXXL. Of course they've all chosen to be twelve years of age in order to fit into their favorite costumes and masks."

"Twelve, I don't think that's a good idea at all. Bugs, I mean boys that age hate girls," said Mary.

"That's what they want you to believe, Girlfriend," said Marta. "Go upstairs and see for yourself. Just name the one you find suitable."

"Maybe I'll give them all names," said Mary and headed for the door.

"Hey wait," said the ladybug, "don't you want to choose a costume and a mask?"

"No, for once I just want me to be me, and hope for the best," replied Mary.

"O-*kay*," said Marta, staring evenly at her, "good luck. You best get an early start then."

~5~
Room 108

Mary eyed the three keys in her hand. They were of drastically different types. The strangest to her was the one marked only "master key." Since the other two had numbers she assumed this key must be for room 108. It had four rows of teeth set at 90 degrees to each other around a central shaft.

"Hmmm," reflected Mary, "108. That must be on the ground floor." So she went through the big double doors and proceeded down a long hall. It was a long haul before she even got to any rooms with any room in them. There were all sorts of storerooms, pantries, cupboards and closets to pass first. None of them were marked so she had to open each one to find out if it was a guest room or just a storeroom, pantry, cupboard or closet. The master key in her hand opened every door.

Finally she got to the rooms with numbers carved on little wooden plaques above the doors. Yes, good. 1, 2, 3, 4. But wait a minute. Where were the rooms numbered one hundred and higher? Then she remembered. Silly her. In Europe the first floor is called the ground floor and the second floor is called the first floor. And this being a *French* house, and this being the ground floor, well the numbers would be in the single digits. She'd have to go up one story to find the one hundreds. Up to the first floor. Clear as mud pie?

This she did and after a similar but even longer, and more frustrating row of storerooms, pantries, cupboards and closets, she came at last to room 108. Having the key, she naturally opened the door and barged right in.

"Whoa!" burst a husky voice from somewhere close. "U dun need tuh make up my room till I'm out uh duh bath! And knock first next time. K?"

Mary looked all around the room but no one could be seen. So she impishly closed the door with a click, and still in the room, perched herself daintily on a straight-backed chair by the door.

Barely a minute passed before a huge body all covered in soap suds streaked from the bathroom, across the oriental rug, and into the walk-in closet. It looked like a huge cotton ball. It ran so fast, it left a trail of bubbles swirling in its wake.

A few minutes later a wide-eyed carpenter ant emerged and stared at Mary sitting self-consciously in her chair. "G, wuh yuh here all along? R yuh here tuh C A real working man?" The ant was wearing bib overalls, two pairs of big boots, and one pair of leather work gloves.

Mary just smiled sweetly at him. "Could this be my prince-apparent?" she thought to herself.

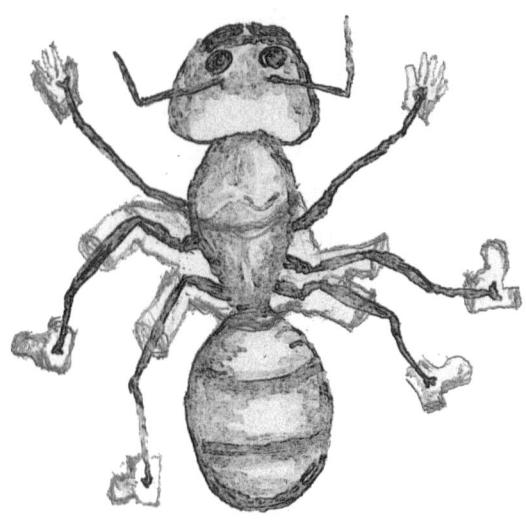

"Confounded bottle of shower soap," he continued. "Y, the more U use, the more annoying it gets."

"It's bubble bath," said Mary. "You wouldn't know anything about that. It's for girls only. How did you get it?"

"O, it was A gift," he said, "A practical joke, I C."

"I see," said Mary, "but not from me. Tell me why you should be my prince-apparent."

"Because I C U R A QT. And because I'm the only man in this house who does any real work. Manly work. C my hard hat and tool belt?"

Mary did not think she was a cutie, so she frowned at him.

She was impressed, however, to see the hard hat and the tool belt full of imposing things like hammers, pliers, and wood files. Why he needed three tape measures, she was afraid to ask. Probably one to measure up, one to measure down, and one to measure sideways. The cloth one she used in dressmaking was more handy because it could also measure *around* things. The workman was proud of how many nails he carried in his tool belt pocket. Mary thought this was a silly thing to be proud of. It didn't carry that many anyway. Her pin cushion in the sewing room had way many more than that.

The workman did let her try on his hard hat and she was surprised at how light it was. Nothing at all like a football helmet. And it didn't even have a faceguard. So far, she wasn't that impressed with the workman. That is until he showed her his steel toed work boots. They had metal under the leather toes so you could hit them with a hammer and it wouldn't hurt. Why she could even stand on them, which she did. They even danced around the floor a bit until a Henry F. Phillips screwdriver started poking her in the stomach.

"Why do you have so many tools?" she asked.

"Because of the code," he replied. Everything has to be built to code, and all carpenters have to live by this code as well."

What code?" she asked.

The Carpenters' Code," he said.

1. Carry as many tools as you can.

2. Make sure they are sharp.

3. Make sure they look greasy or paint stained.

4. Make sure they are cordless.

5. Measure twice before you cut anything.

6. Glue back anything you cut by mistake.

7. Wear heavy boots and a concerned look.

8. Don't assume that anything is square or plumb.

9. Don't assume that ladies know anything.

10. Never forget your lunchbox.

"Wanna C my T square or skill saw?" he asked.

"So what can you do with all this skill?" she demanded point blank. "What can you make for me?"

"By day," he replied, "I work at A construction job. At night I have to put all my tired feet up in front of the TV, but on weekends, when it's not football, basketball or baseball season, I can B a builder for you. I want 2 make the Q-test little house you ever saw."

"How long would that take?" she asked politely.

"Doesn't matter," he said, "when I finish we can sell it and start on another. I'm a fixer-uper kind of guy. I'm the 'do it yourself' man. You look strong, why don't you come do it with me for A while?"

"Just for a while?" asked Mary.

"Well, you know how it is nowadays. I'm a fix-her-uper kind of guy. I'm the 'do it for yourself' man. When I'm finished fixing you up, it's time to start on another. Wanna dance on my toes again?"

Mary frowned again at the carpenter ant. "Well I suppose I must give you a name before leaving," she said. "Let's see – how about Mister McBum?"

With this she stormed out of the room and slammed the door. Mister McBum is still wondering why. He went to the mirror and adjusted his mask. It is the mask of male superiority in mechanical things. That means he was trying to tell himself that boys can work with tools better than girls. Do you think that's true?

Mary was disappointed that the carpenter ant seemed more interested in the tools in his belt than in her.

"Oh well," she sighed, "there's always room number 214," and she headed up the stairs once again.

~6~
Room 214

Mary eyed the two keys left in her hand. They were of drastically different types. The smaller of the two was marked "do not duplicate." This meant it had to be very important. If you took it to a hardware store they would refuse to make a copy of it for you. Even if you had ready cash to pay for it. It was stamped 214. It had only one row of teeth but they were very long and sharp.

"Hmmm," reflected Mary, "214. That must be on the American third floor. The European second floor." So up the staircase she went and proceeded down yet another long hall. It was an even longer haul before she got to any real rooms. There were all sorts of storerooms, pantries, cupboards and closets to pass first. This time she didn't open them because the key in her hand didn't fit.

Finally she got to the rooms with numbers carved on little wooden plaques above the doors. Yes, good. 201, 202, 203, 204. After quite a walk she came at last to room 214. This time she knocked politely even though she had a key.

"I can't hear you!" burst a husky voice from somewhere inside.

This seemed odd to Mary, since he most certainly *had* heard her or else he wouldn't have replied as he did. Nevertheless, she knocked again, louder this time.

"I can't *hear* you!" burst the booming voice from inside.

This time Mary pounded on the door with her whole forearm.

"That's better," bellowed the voice, "come in, its not locked."

Mary entered and there, standing, blocking her way was a tall, barrel-chested army ant general. His ribbons and decorations made his chest stick out even more. "Could this be my prince-apparent?" she thought to herself.

"I always have an 'Open Door Policy,'" he roared.

This seemed strange to Mary since his door was closed. But he continued shouting at her, "That means that anyone under my command can come in here and talk to me. And since I'm a general, *everyone* is under my command."

"Do you have to yell at everyone?" asked Mary politely.

"Apparently I do. Nobody listens to me anymore," came the reply.

Mary just smiled sweetly at him.

"Wipe that smile off your face," he said, "we're at war."

"What? You and me," said Mary, "I don't think so. Are we?"

"We are at war with the forces of fanatical-extremism everywhere. Are you with me, or not?" Mary looked puzzled, so he added, "Fanatical-extremism means believing so strongly about something that you go around killing babies and bystanders just to prove your point."

"Oh I see," said Mary, putting her hand to her mouth, "that's a noble cause. Then tell me why you should be my prince-apparent."

"Because you'd make a smart-looking soldier and because I'm the only man in this house who does any worthwhile work. Honorable work. Shooting and stabbing people. It's a dirty job, but someone has to do it. See my pistol and my sword?"

Mary did not think she was smart-looking so she frowned at him.

She did, however, notice the pistol and the sword neatly strapped to his belt. Why he needed three pairs of binoculars, she was afraid to ask. Probably one to see up, one to see down, and one to see sideways. The three-way mirror she used in dressmaking was more handy because it could also see *around* things. The general was proud of how many bullets for his pistol he had in his belt. Mary thought this was a silly thing to be proud of. There weren't that many anyway. She had many more spools of thread for her sewing machine than that.

The general did let her try on his combat helmet and she was surprised at how heavy it was. Nothing at all like a football helmet. And it didn't even have a faceguard. He called it a "steel pot."

So far, she wasn't that impressed with the general. That is until he showed her his Zipper Desert Stryker Combat boots. They had laces as usual, but also a zipper down the side so you could get them off quickly when it was bedtime. They looked big and clumsy, but he said he could run, jump and even dance in them. So they danced around the floor a bit until one of the silver oak leaf clusters on his Army Commendation metal started catching on her sweater.

"Wanna see my M203 grenade launcher?" he asked. "I can blow away a rabbit at 300 meters."

"Why would you want to do that?" she demanded point blank. "What can a grenade launcher launcherer do for me?"

"It's not the weapons," he replied, "but the man that handles them. By day, I work fighting the wars, protecting you from fanatics, heretics and lunatics. At night I have to put my tired feet up in front of the TV, but on weekends, when there's no athletics, I can pitch for you the sweetest little army pup tent you ever saw. I'm the father of all battlefield romantics."

"Just how big would a pup tent be?" she asked politely.

"Doesn't matter," he said, "all we do is sleep in it. I'm an on-the-go kind of guy. I'm the 'been-there done-that' man. You look game, why don't you come along with me to the war-games?"

"In a pup tent?" asked Mary.

"Well, you know how it is in these times. I'm a 'keep-advancing' kind of guy. I'm the 'defeat everything in sight' man. When I'm finished conquering with you, it's time to envelope the next objective. So are you ready to charge ahead and blow things up with me for awhile?"

Why do you have to blow everything up?" she asked.

"Because it's in the Soldiers Code of Conduct." He said.

The Soldiers Code of Conduct:

1. If it moves, shoot it.
2. If it's in your way, blow it up.
3. If you can't blow it up, paint it.
4. If it's wearing a uniform, salute it.
5. If it's a weapon, clean it.
6. If it's a bigger weapon than yours, get it.
7. If it comes on a mess tray, eat it.
8. If it's litter on the ground, pick it up.
9. If it has moving parts, take it apart.

10. If it's made out of paper, file it.

Mary frowned again at the army ant. She didn't think much of his Code of Conduct. "Well I suppose I must give you a name before leaving," she said. "Let's see – how about Mister McBomb.

With this she stormed out of the room and slammed the door in his face. Mister McBomb, I mean *General* McBomb is still wondering why. He went to the mirror and adjusted his mask. His is the mask of male dominance in conquering territory. That means he was trying to tell himself that soldiers can defeat the enemy better than soldierettes. Do you think that's true?

Mary was disappointed that the army ant seemed more interested in the bullets in his belt than in her.

"Oh well," she sighed, "there's always room number 401 and she headed up the stairs once again. Only this time she was in for a surprise.

~7~

Finding Room 401

Mary eyed the only key left in her hand. It was the biggest key by far, an old-fashioned skeleton key. It was very fancy with a long, cylindrical shank made of heavy, dull bronze. Its bit was rectangular, but jagged and square-looking at the end. Stamped deeply on its bow was the number 401.

"Hmmm," reflected Mary, "401. That must be on the fifth floor." But wait a minute, the château only had three floors, and she was on that floor already! So she walked around and around looking for a solution to her problem. She even found a trapdoor and went up into the attic but it was scary, disgusting, and disappointingly empty. No guest rooms up there. Not even a bat or a ghost. Do you believe in ghosts? Mary does, but I need to talk to her about that.

So she went back down to the third story, which in this story is the second floor. There she began to cry because it seemed there was no prince-apparent for her, none at least who didn't smoke or ride a horse.

Suddenly she heard a familiar voice coming from half-behind a light fixture on the wall. "S-why yous steerie sighed, Smary?"

"Sbeg your spardon?" replied Mary.

"Don'st sue snow your Shcandelaria?" said Mary's favorite little spider-friend.

"Oh, syme sorry," said Mary, "you've grown so smuch. Sand your legs are longer."

"So s-why the sweeping? Sgimme a sug," said her shiny black buddy.

"So, Shcandelaria," cried Mary, "sue snow sigh scant stew sugs yet. Syme just snot ready. Sits snot sue. Sits sme. But syme sweeping because sigh scant find my sway stew room 401. Sit smite just salve suh man of my streams sin there."

The spider thought for a moment, then said, "Salve sue seen the strap store stew the central tower sattic? The central tower has four floors. 401s sin there. Swill sue scum wisimi? Yessie, scum! Scum! Scum!"

"Oh, stop sit," said Mary laughing, "of course I'll scum."

So the two friends headed off together into the highest tower of the château. To keep on the safe side, they followed the almost invisible silk strands that spiders call "the narrow way." At the trapdoor,

Shcandelaria said, "Sup sue must sgo. Sigh scant. Sits snot swear spiders are swelcome. Snow narrow sway sup there."

So Mary thanked the spider and they made plans to meet again very soon. Then Mary did something quite unexpected, even to herself. She picked Shcandelaria up in her arms, and being very careful not to break off any of her legs, gave her a great big hug and even a little kiss on the forehead just above her five eyes.

"So thank sue, Smary, but please snow suckings with the slips. That's the sway we sweet, remembers?"

"Syme so sorry," said Mary, "sigh forgot. See ya slater then?"

"Soaky dokie, sin a few sours." said the spider and disappeared into a crack in the wall.

Getting back to the business at hand, Mary pushed tentatively at the trap door at the top of the stairs. Nothing happened so she pushed harder and the plywood gave way with an eerie creak. There were no hinges, it just lifted free from the hole in the ceiling. So Mary quietly shoved it aside and scrambled quickly though the opening before she could lose her nerve.

Fortunately, the first thing she saw was a light switch, and happily it worked. Sure enough there were no spiders nor cobwebs to be seen. In fact everything was painted a glossy white. Quite odd for an attic, especially an attic in a tower. Well actually it was more of an ivory color. And more of a satin finish, rather than glossy. Inside the ivory tower were only two rooms, 401 and 402. No room for any storerooms, pantries, cupboards or closets. Since Mary was sure they could never get a horse all the way up here, the gentleman in 402 must be a smoker. A quick whiff under the door told her she was right. Maybe he would be okay, she thought. Maybe he doesn't inhale. But then why smoke at all she wondered. And she would certainly have to inhale *his* smoke. Still, think of all the people who live with dogs and breathe their disgusting dog-breath day in and day out.

"Oh, don't be silly," she exclaimed out loud, and rapped politely on the room 401 door next door.

~8~
Room 401

Mary knocked again on the door to room 401. She had come so far and now it appeared there was no one home. Then suddenly there was a faint mumbling from within.

"I'm deep in thought," came the voice. It was a creaky, creepy voice with an edge of irritation to it. "Use your key."

This Mary did and the old-fashioned key opened the old-fashioned lock in the old-fashioned door, emitting her into a very old-fashioned room. The room was furnished with a desk, two chairs, one on either side of the desk and a single floor lamp. Bookcases filled each wall from floor to ceiling with old, dusty volumes of all shapes and sizes. Behind the desk sat an odd little creature garbed in a black academic robe and a mortarboard cap. He looked very old-fashioned himself. He was wearing thick, rimless spectacles and had a very long, pointy nose to hold them up. There were three velvet chevrons on the sleeves of his gown and a velvet facing ran down the front. The mortarboard hat was flat and square with a silly-looking, silk tassel suspended from a button in the top center of the board. The bright yellow tassel swished across the face of the little man whenever his head moved. This seemed to irritate him, but he just kept brushing it aside.

Did I say man? I meant to say booklouse.

Yes, he was indeed a booklouse, widely regarded as voracious devourers of books and all sorts of scholarly papers. Sometimes they have even been known to consume the wooden shelves the books come on. For that they have big buck teeth and even bigger stomachs. Otherwise, they just look like an ant. "Could this be my prince-apparent?" she thought to herself.

"Don't call me a booklouse," said the booklouse gruffly, glancing up at Mary as if he could read her mind. "How would you like to be called a louse. No? I didn't think so. So there!"

"Then what *should* I call you?" asked Mary.

"You may refer to me as Liposcelis bostrychophila, although my personal name is Professor Bookworm Ant Emeritus. You may address me simply as Professor Ant."

"But you're not an ant," protested Mary.

"Why do you think I wear this long robe? It will be our little secret, okay? I'd much rather be an ant than a louse," said the louse. "Wouldn't *you*?"

"So what does emeritus mean?" asked Mary, folding her hands in front of her.

"Emeritus means I'm a person of merit," said the Professor, "and therefore you must call me by my title, even though I'm not really entitled to it anymore."

"Why aren't you entitled to your title? Were you naughty?"

"No, I wasn't naughty," hissed the louse, "I just retired that's all. Although that is a misleading term. In retirement years one just becomes busier than ever catching up on the real work that one was too busy to catch up on years ago."

Now Mary could see why Marta had called this the room of last resort. This bug must be 112 years old, not twelve.

"Oh, I'm really twelve," he said, as if he could read her mind. "I'm just pretending to be old so I can get respect. But it doesn't seem to be working. Maybe I'm overdoing it a bit, do you think? No one admires gray hair anymore. Except gray squirrels, of course, and gray foxes."

"So what are you so busy at, up here?" asked Mary.

"Well, if you must know, I'm rewriting the biographies of all the famous ants in history. Did you know that you people claimed that many famous personages were humans, when they were really ants! Either that or louses."

"How shocking," said Mary, "so who are these people who were really ants."

"Well there's Mark Ant-ony, for one," began the professor. "Also I'm doing a paper on Mickey M-ant-le and of course, Aunt Jemima. And something else really shocking – the Beatles were louses."

"Well, I never knew they were louses," confessed Mary. "It's good that you're writing a book. I'm impressed. So tell me why you should be my prince-apparent."

"Well because you'd make an eye-fetching librarian and because I'm the only man in this house who does any worthwhile work. Scholarly work. Writing and rewriting history. It's a thankless job, but someone has to do it. Would you like to touch my tassel?"

Mary did not think she was eye-fetching, so she frowned at him.

She had no desire to touch his tassel. And why he needed three fountain pens, she was afraid to ask. Probably one to write things down, one to fix them up, and one to cross them out. The tailors chalk she used in sewing was more handy because it could also be easily erased. The professor was proud of how many little buttons ran down the front of his long and flowing robe. Mary thought this was a silly thing to be proud of. There weren't that many buttons anyway. Not compared to the number on the many ladies' dresses she had made, and the many she had already worn – although today she was wearing bootcut jeans and an old sweater.

The professor did let her try on his mortarboard cap, and she was surprised at how awkward it was. Nothing at all like a football helmet. And it didn't even have a faceguard to contend with. So far, she wasn't that impressed with the professor. That is until he showed her his briarwood rocker ink blotter and matching box.

The set was expertly crafted, finely polished to bring out the wood grain, and everything was topped off with a sizeable, solid brass knob. "Would you like to try it out?" he asked. So she blotted several papers until the ink started getting on her fingers and then all over her sweater.

"Would you care to see my doctorial dissertation?" he asked. "Nowadays that's just a fancy word for 'book report.' I wrote it on George Washington's teeth."

"Why would you want to write about that?" she demanded. "What can an expert on George Washington's teeth do for me?"

"All the other subjects were taken," he whined, "but it's fascinating. Did you know that he had such bad teeth that all the dentists could do was take them out one by one. Finally he had a full set of false teeth made from a hippopotamus tusk and a cow's tooth. They were carved by hand, and held in his mouth by little metal springs. Being somewhat large for his mouth, they created a peculiar expression on his face, which can be seen in many of his portraits.

"Still, it's not the subject that matters, young girl. You can write about anything nowadays. Its how well we impress others with our big words. And how preposterous our conclusions are. For instance, I claim that our first president didn't make longer speeches because his dentures got in the way, and even broke and fell out from time to time. If he had made longer speeches he could have persuaded the British to give up and go home. Out of sheer boredom, if for no other reason. Then we wouldn't have had to fight the

Revolutionary War and today we could have a queen. Just like the ants."

"As a historian, aren't you just supposed to stick to the facts?" asked Mary.

"No," he said, "we have a strict code to write by."

Historians code:

1. Write only about what really happened.
2. or what probably happened.
3. or what could have happened.
4. or what you wish had happened.
5. or what would be funny if it had happened.
6. or what would be embarrassing if it happened.
7. or what nobody else has said has happened.
8. or what shouldn't have happened.
9. or what should have happened to somebody else.
10. or whatever you happen to write about, really.

Professor Ant saw that Mary was getting antsy herself, so he got back to the point of the conversation. "Anyway, you ask what I can do for you, my dear? Well, by day, I work thinking up new things that have never been thought up before. Then at night I have to put my tired brain up in front of the TV. But on weekends, when there's no college games to watch, I will write for you the sweetest little sonnets you ever saw. I mean read."

"And what would you say in the sonnets? I mean write." she asked politely.

"Doesn't matter," he said, "as long as the words are beautiful and well, impress. I'm a creative kind of guy. I'm the 'do something new' man. You look intelligent, why don't you come along with me and be my inspiration?"

"Join you in a sonnet? A fantasy world?" asked Mary.

"Hey, you're in one already, missy. And you know how it is in this day and age. I'm a 'make your own truth' kind of guy. I'm the 'virtual reality' man. When you don't inspire me anymore, it's time to move on to new motivation elsewhere. So, are you ready to forge ahead and create new memories together?"

Mary frowned again at Professor Ant. He was really turning out to be a louse. "Well I suppose I must give you a name before leaving," she said. "Let's see – how about Mister McDumb."

With this she stormed out of the room and slammed the door in his face. Mister, I should say *Professor* McDumb is still wondering why. He went to the mirror and adjusted his mask. His is the mask of male dominance in mature intellectual pursuits. That means he was trying to tell himself that men can read and write better books than women. Do you think that's true?

Mary was disappointed that the woodlouse seemed more interested in the buttons on his robe than in her.

"Oh well," she sighed, "there's always room number…"

"Oops," she murmured, "looks like I've run out of rooms, and out of luck. Out of hope too, I guess." So not wanting to settle for a man that smelled of smoke, or horse, or worse, she actually remembered me. Good thing I had showered that day long ago before going up to rescue her. In desperation she sat down and penned a little letter. A note really. In elegant, tiny handwriting, it spoke cryptically:

Willy, find me at Smary@ChâteauChic.com

Then she went out and wedged it half-through a front window of Mousumerset Manor. Fat chance it would ever be found. And even fatter chance I'd ever be interested in seeing her again. I would probably be married. Or dead. (Little did she know.)

So after returning to the Château she just sat down right there in the middle of the hall and sobbed and sobbed. But don't worry my little children. God never leaves His children alone for longer than they can stand it. Soon Mary would be in for an even greater adventure.

~9~
The Virtual Cottage

Mary was laying on her side in a pool of tears. When she stopped weeping long enough to look around she spied something very interesting. Across the floor, in a corner at the end of the hall was the tiniest little cottage you could ever imagine. It had but one room, three windows, one door, and one chimney for the one fireplace. Of course no real fires were

allowed because this was really just a toy cottage inside a toy château, inside a toy manor house. But when you're inside this book everything becomes real, right?

Naturally right now you're wondering the same thing that Mary wondered. Could she go *inside* this cottage? Unfortunately it was only the size of the eraser on the end of a pencil. She couldn't even fit her little finger into it, which she tried by the way. Several times. She peeped inside, then peered inside. She could almost see the tiny fireplace. In front of it was a frail-looking rocking chair and a big, overstuffed recliner. Not really 'big,' mind you. You know what I mean. On the oak paneled wall was an odd-looking photograph of what looked like the diamond out of someone's ring. Only it didn't come to a point at the bottom; it was more like a ball with many flat sides all the way around it. It was clear like a diamond and inside, as if floating, was a distinctly discernable smiley face. It gave Mary the willies, so she stopped staring at it. To one side she saw a metal table with a very large computer on it. It was a desktop computer with a 24 inch flat panel monitor and a nifty optical mouse. The mouse pad had a green tree frog design that said, "Hang in there, the Lord is coming back." Mary had no idea what that meant. She had been told that Jesus had died once and for all on the cross. Then why would he need to come back? Next to the mouse pad was a half empty cup of chai tea.

"Somebody needs to come back and finish their tea," thought Mary. "*Somebody?*" Then it dawned on her. Someone must be living in this cottage. Someone very,

very small. Now she wanted to get inside more than ever.

Well, as you know, nothing can deter determination. Yes, the door was locked; yes, the window was latched; and yes, even the flue in the fireplace was closed. Mary stared at the cottage and then bowed her head in frustration. As she did, her long, straight hair brushed over the cottage roof and cascaded across the front door and doorstep. This gave her an idea. She picked up a tuft of the hair and carefully separated out a single strand. Then, as if threading a needle, she poked the end of it deftly through the front door keyhole.

Of course the hair shrank to the scale of the cottage, but as it went in, so did the fingers that were holding it. And so also did the hand attached to the fingers, and the arm attached to the hand, and the shoulder attached to the arm. You get what I'm saying, right? She, all of her, ended up inside the cottage. Squeezing right through the tiny key hole. Once again, there seemed to be no ill effects to all this shrinking and growing again. In fact, she did rather enjoy being much less than one millimeter tall. For one thing she seemed much stronger, and also she could jump much higher – although her head kept hitting the ceiling annoyingly.

It didn't take her long to explore the one-room cottage. Oddly enough it had no kitchen or bathroom. "Oh well," she thought, "in the olden days the bathroom was outside in an outhouse, and in modern days I'm told everybody eats out in restaurants."

The only thing she hadn't seen from the window was the enormous bed tucked right under it. It had a lovely, soft comforter and a big down pillow. Mary was tired so she took her shoes off and got right in.

"Why are you wearing your bert in shed?" whispered a creepy voice into her ear. It was coming from underneath the covers!

Instantly Mary was out of the bed and even getting back into her shoes.

"Oh don't leave. It's just me. I'm not a mad ban. I just teep all the slime. I won't eat you. In fact I don't eat *anything*. That's why I don't have a bitchen, or a kathroom for that matter. Here let me roll out and introduce myself."

This he did, saying, "Vick Cyrus, at your service."

Mary noticed that he was the 'thing' in the picture on the wall. Yes, Vick Cyrus looked like a ball-shaped diamond with a smiley face floating inside which kept turning around to always face her.

"I'm glad you cropped into my dotage," it said, "I'll be your guest during your stay here."

Mary, mindful of her manners, said, "Oh, but I'm the guest, you're the host."

"Hot near, Sweetie," smiled the smiley face, "in here everything is either backwards, upside-down or steal range. In fact, in order to get this small, you just jumped ahead forty years in your time. But not to worry, you're still dung and ye-lightful here. Tech-spackular!"

Mary began to feel uncomfortable and wondered if she should leave. But the smiley face looked so friendly, and the 'diamond' around it so mesmerizing, that she eventually took a seat on the edge of the overstuffed chair.

"Bean lack and put your feet up," said Vick Cyrus. "Don't be afraid."

Mary just perched where she was, stared at him and wondered why he talked so funny.

"Don't be toe sense," he said. "Get low. You have to be lax before you can relax. I won't eat you. Would you like some belly jeans, or some nixed mutts? In fact, and if you moat dined, it's time for me to go online for a while and free with my bends."

With this the 'diamond' rolled over to the computer keyboard and after staring at it for a few moments, began to cry. "Who-boo," it wailed somewhat unconvincingly. "As you can sanely plea, I have no arms and fingers like yourself with which to control the mouse and keyboard. Would you mind coming over and hending a land?"

This Mary did because she was uneasy in the easy chair, and she had always heard how wonderful the internet was. This proved to be an understatement, as you will plainly see in the next chapter.

~10~
The Avatar

"Push this, click that, scroll down, hit the back button," it was Vick Cyrus helping Mary navigate her way into the internet. "You know what," he said after ten minutes of these tedious instructions, "why don't you just wear me in a ring. Then I can control your fingers directly. It would be so much easier and faster for you, for me, and for both of us."

Mary thought this might be a good idea so she asked if he happened to have any ring settings laying around, preferably 14 carat gold. Give gold to a girl and she'll do anything for you. The carrot and the stick approach always motivated Mary, especially the carat part.

"Oh certainly," laughed the smiley face, "a setting just your size is in that drawer." His eyes glanced down to a small drawer in the computer desk.

So Mary opened it and found a single silver solitaire setting just her size. Hmm, all that glitters is not gold. She of course put it on anyway and Cyrus jumped right in and made himself at home. "Diamonds are forever," he exclaimed, "I like it here." At first, this made her finger a little numb but never mind, instantly she was whizzing around the internet and discovering all sorts of amazing websites. Her fingers seemed to know just where to go and how to double-click and even triple-click with ease. She could even download her favorite music and pictures to her desktop for future use.

After about an hour of this, her fingers led her instinctively not just to a chat room, but to a whole cyber world with music, sound effects, realistic scenery and lots of people just like herself inside. They were all wearing big diamond rings like hers, with smiley faces in them.

One, dressed only in a knife and a loincloth to carry it in, looked realistically like Tarzan. He came up to her and said, "Me Tarzan, you who?"

"I'm Mary," said Mary, gazing dead on into his muscular, manly chest. "I'm glad to be hair... I mean *here*," she said.

"Mary! How boring," said the jungle-man. "Why don't you be a Jane and I'll swing you off through the trees?"

"What about the real Jane?" protested the girl. "Besides, I don't want to wear costumes or masks anymore." Mary noticed that Tarzan's chest hair was pasted on with rubber cement. She hoped that *he* wouldn't turn out to be her prince-apparent.

"Not a mask," said the ape-man. "In here you can't just be a plain-Jane like yourself; you need an avatar."

"Where can I get that?" asked Mary.

"I got mine from the guy over there wearing a sheet," said Tarzan. "His are free and they have a thirty day money back guarantee, he says."

"But wait," began Mary, scrunching her eyebrows. But Tarzan was already man-handling her over to the holy man.

The holy man was thin, bent-over and bare-chested. "I am The Most Reverend Doctor Hadji Swami Guru Monk-Lama, RN, NCAA," he said. Then he just stood there as if expecting Mary to bow or kneel or something.

"It is customary to kiss my ring," he said. His ring was identical to Mary's so she wondered why he shouldn't kiss hers instead.

Instead she asked, "What's an avatar? Your holifullness."

"Oh, you mean avatara, from the Sanskrit अवतार. In here, my girl-child, an avatara, is more than a representation of yourself. It is more than your ambassador to a foreign country. It is more than your piece on the Monopoly board of life. It *is*, my dear, in fact, an actual incarnation of yourself. An embodiment. It is *you*. But the *you* you always wanted to be. The *you* you could never achieve in the real world. The *you* that you can finally love."

"But I don't want to love myself," said Mary.

"Well I can plainly see why," said the swami. "That's the whole reason for avataras. Hmm. Let's see. To begin with you need to be taller, tanner and entirely more, well, figurative, would you call it? Overly and necessarily so. And your face needs to look like a celebrity's. Certainly yes. I have a file of them right here to choose from."

"But I want to use my own face," insisted Mary.

"Just wait," said the swami.

After a few mouse clicks, yes the old man was on a computer, (computers were everywhere), Mary's avatar was finished. And my, was it ever striking. It was still Mary, but also someone from the movies. A heroine, someone you loved, but her name escapes you, as did she, to your everlasting sorrow. Even Mary herself had to love it, and it became her nicely. I mean it *became* her. Literally. Mary *became* her avatar and walked away from the swami, and even Tarzan, like someone who had just won an academy award and all the money, fame and good fortune that comes with it. At least that was what Mary thought as she strutted away, head held high, hair and hips swinging in synchronous, complementary circles behind her.

"Where are you going?" pleaded Tarzan after her.

"To find, at last, a prince-apparent who is apparently worthy of me," she snapped back over her shoulder.

"Well, I doubt if you can find better than me," yelled Tarzan, adjusting his knife.

But in the end, as you will see, Mary would do just that.

~11~
The Chat Room

Mary's fingers, or should I say the ring on her finger, ushered her into a special chat room called "fancy friends." It was tastefully done with a central open room for mingling, dominated by a giant diamond chandelier, each stone lit by a glowing smiley face. Around the edge of the great room were many inviting alcoves behind curtains where apparently you could be alone with the prince or princess of your choice. All this was supposed to help you meet fancy people who would fancy you in return. Instantly. No laborious small talk, or expensive giving of gifts or spending countless hours sharing favorite frills or family foibles. Just instant friendship or even more.

"Could I find my prince-apparent in here?" she thought to herself. She even noted she was already wearing an engagement ring of sorts – that is, if she could learn to ignore the silly funny face always gawking at her from deep within it. Her ring finger was truly numb now, but that was little price to pay for the fun and adventure the ring was bringing her.

Just inside the door of the chat room was a dropdown box which asked Mary to enter what type of person she is: boy/girl; age; hair/eye/skin/favorite color; hobbies/hobby-horses; best/worst subject in school; taste in music/food/ movies; other things she liked, and the like. She was also prompted to provide a photo of her avatar. Next she was asked about her desired prince. Height/weight/sex and all that. Lots of other stuff too. Of course she hoped this would describe the real guy she wanted, and not his avatar. But she'd have to settle for his avatar, she supposed. "Funny," she thought, "two avatars falling in love. Certainly they'd fall in love; they were perfect embodiments of all their pent-up dreams. Wow, a daydream marriage." Her insides quivered. And the smiley face on her finger smiled.

One last question was asked: Do you want to chat with an internet predator? The worst predators she could think of were lions, tigers and bears so she clicked "yes" reasoning that they had many qualities she admired in men. Most girls click "no" but it made little difference. Most lions, tigers and bears have little regard for the truth when filling out forms in chat rooms.

Finally she had to check "agree" to the

chat room code of conduct.

1. No yelling
2. No bad language
3. No peeking into other alcoves
4. No bringing in outside food

5. No cameras or tape recorders

6. No off-topic or off-color discussions

7. Keep your hands to yourself

8. Pay by the hour and in advance

9. No refunds, no returns

10. No guarantees of satisfaction

Soon a popup box appeared above an alcove across the room. It said "Mary" in flashing red letters. Nervously Mary adjusted her outfit and pinched her cheeks to get a bit more color in them. She began to wonder if a mask might not have been a better idea than using her own face like this. "Too late now," she reflected. So she strode confidently across the grand carpet and up to her alcove. There was an inviting light shining through the curtain.

"What if a lion or a tiger or a bear appears?" she fretted. But when she entered, her very own "prince" popped up inside, surprisingly not in the form of a lion, but a lion *tamer*. Actually lion tamers don't actually *tame* lions. They just trick them to do tricks, give them food and water, and sweep out their cages from time to time. This particular lion tamer wore fitted, white pants, black boots, a red jacket with gold buttons, and a toothy smile. He carried a big, black whip and a straight back, wooden chair with thick teeth marks decorating its legs. He had short hair and shifty eyes. Mary's avatar was immediately impressed, but the man motioned her not to enter the cage he was in.

Suddenly several large, hungry lions entered through a trap door in the floor. Their hides looked like thick carpet, but they moved as if they were clothed in the sheerest silk. There were three females and one magnificent male with all the might and mane of the king of beasts. Mary's fingers longed to bury themselves in his long hair and pull her up astride his back. But her knees felt too weak to even get her near the cage.

The lion tamer went over to this great cat and thrust the chair in his face. The lion let out a great roar, but obediently jumped up on a tiny pedestal like his three well-trained sisters. After this, the lionesses did a series of tricks including sitting up, rolling over, begging, and jumping through hoops. One of them even let the lion tamer pet her like a kitten, and put a cutesy white baby bonnet on her.

Then, with his whip cracking at their ears, he herded the three sleek females back down the trap door and closed it securely. While he was doing this, the great male growled and swiped a paw at his back. But the man seemed unconcerned, contemptuous even of the big cat. He turned and stared into its huge, yellow eyes.

Presently he motioned for Mary to enter the cage. Mary looked astounded, then looked down at the sawdust around her feet. Her feet seemed entirely too small and delicate to be entering lion cages. Her toes tried to crinkle up within her shoes.

"Mary!" bellowed the lion tamer, "while you're young! The lion awaits you. Don't display any fear, are you not the 'queen of beasts?'"

Something stirred inside her and at once she knew she could not only enter the cage, but control the lion as well. It would eat from her hand, lick her cheek, playfully muss her hair. That's what she told herself anyway. Why, she would end up riding the thing around the ring, she mused. At night it would protect her from all manner of attackers; its paw would be her pillow, its mane her blanket.

It roared again as she opened the cage and entered. Its flashing white teeth challenged her courage, but her tiny feet stood firm. She took a step forward but a low growl sent her back against the bars. The thick, black-tipped tail waved to and fro, as the doublewide nostrils gathered in her scent. The lion's ears folded back and his huge yellow eyes devoured her own small green ones.

Then the lion tamer emitted a low guttural laugh and, all the while holding the now terrified Mary against the bars with a stare, slowly backed out of the cage. With a huge padlock, he locked the gate behind him and walked out a side door. The lion eyed Mary deliciously and took a step off his little pedestal.

~12~
The Smiley Meal

The lion bounded over to the defenseless girl and slashed at her dress with his claws. For a moment she was buried beneath his great body, but then he grabbed her hair in his jaws and swung her ruthlessly into the air. She landed stiff and hard, and again he tore at her dress, ripping it to shreds this time. She screamed. She screamed again and again but this only egged the beast on and soon he had her leg off and flying across the floor and under the next table. The poor girl tried in vain to push him away but succeeded only in spilling her coke. The coke ran across the table and onto her brothers pants, which cooled his enthusiasm considerably.

"Now look what you've done," he whined.

But the girl was not interested in the coke mess. She was scurrying under the next table to retrieve her poor doll's leg. Everybody in the restaurant was staring at them, so the boy sheepishly put his lion back into his smiley meal box. "They shouldn't put toys in smiley meals if we're not allowed to play with them," he said to no one in particular.

I of course, rushed out as soon as I could from behind the counter to see what my sister's grandkids were getting into this time. It was embarrassing because I was the assistant manager of the restaurant, and dangerous because the new head manager was due in to work at any time. There was coke all over the floor to clean up and shrieking kids to calm. I pulled the crying girl from under the table and in the process she spilled the contents of a woman's purse into the aisle. "My leg must be under the other table!" she screamed into the poor woman's ear. Just then an old lady with a cane slipped on the soda-slippery floor and tumbled into a table spilling soup into a gentleman's lap. He was dripping chicken and noodles all over the floor as a waitress was leading him to the bathroom. The lady's cane went flying across the floor and into the shins of a stern-looking man.

Yes, at this exact time the stern-looking manager *did* walk in, only to find me on my hands and knees looking for the lost doll's leg under a table of college girls. "I'm looking for a leg," I said, and they all started giggling and then began screaming in pretend and playful horror.

"Let go of my toe!" yelled one. "Let go of my ankle!" yelled another. One even stood up on her chair.

"William!" the manager was red-faced and bellowing. "Get out from under that table this instant."

"I'm so sorry girls," he said, "nothing like this has ever happened at Frankie's Chicken before. I assure you that this rude man will be fired immediately." The girls tried to tell him that it was all a joke, but they were cackling too hard to make any sense.

So I was hauled off to the backroom, together with Katherine's grandchildren. "Why don't you take these horrible children of yours home," said the manager. "And when you get home, stay home. Don't bother coming back to work again. And, oh, before you go, give me your keys and your cell phone. They belong to the restaurant. You know we don't give second chances to employees grabbing girls' legs under tables."

"You know **the restaurant code:**

1. Never grab girl's legs under tables
2. Never serve leftovers
3. Never serve dogs
4. Never serve dog
5. Never serve anything you wouldn't eat yourself
6. Never clean tables with floor mops
7. Never leave the dishes to soak overnight
8. Never lock the bathrooms
9. Never run out of smiles, smiley meals, or napkins
10. Never complain about the food

I was flabbergasted, for I had worked in this restaurant for over eighteen years without so much as spilling a glass of water. But all I could think to say was, "These aren't my children. I'm single."

Luckily Katherine arrived at this precise instant and claimed them as the product of her eldest son. "Can't I entrust them to you for even an hour while I go shopping?" she snapped at me. Then she turned and addressed the manager.

"Please forgive poor William," she said, "he fell out of a maple tree when he was young and has never been the same since. Actually his brother pushed him out, so it wasn't even his fault. His brother was mean when he was little and killed insects and things with sticks. So naturally he went into the Navy. William here, couldn't get into the Navy, or even the Army, so he works for restaurants."

"That's enough, Katherine," I said, but the manager interrupted.

"You *do* seem to be a good employee, William," he said, "so I will only suspend you from work for one month. Get a good rest and come back ready to behave. So you're still single, huh. Well you'll not find a wife for yourself by crawling under restaurant tables and grabbing legs."

I was so upset at being falsely accused of such a horrible thing that I drove straight home and cried into my pillow. My cat was so upset at seeing a grown man cry that she hid under the bed and missed her supper. I was age fifty, you know. The next morning I finally decided to get out of bed and check my email. Not that I ever got anything but spam trying to sell things. How trying. But my life was such that even spam was interesting. In fact my house was filled with things I didn't need, but had bought out of boredom.

Sure enough, only spam for email. I didn't want a trip to Las Vegas or need any new vitamins. Then there was a message about "fantasy masks and costumes."

You could buy them to wear in a chat room and talk to other nice people in "fantasy masks and costumes." "Ha *ha*," I thought, "I bet the people in there are not nice at all. I bet they're just after my money, what little I have of it."

Just to prove my point I followed the link and sure enough, I had to pay money to get in. Still, there was a scrolling red-letter banner across the top that said "satisfaction guaranteed." How bad could it be? Now that I was suspended from work, I'd have lots of free time on my hands. So what the heck, I went right in.

I'd forgotten I was still dressed in my bathrobe, but as it turned out it didn't matter. I would get a new outfit.

~13~
My Avatar

The first thing that happened to me in the chat room was very pleasant but a bit strange. A striking, young girl with a powdery face, long white legs, and sandaled feet approached. Her toenails were all colors of the rainbow. She gazed at me with big blue eyes behind huge, round, pink-tinted glasses. Her arms were thin and angular, and two antennae stuck out of her jet black hair like an insect's. Or maybe they were part of her wireless earphones. I couldn't tell. She wore a gaudy, silk peasant blouse over a black leather skirt. Smiling sweetly, she slipped a diamond ring on my finger. She had one on hers as well. I hoped this didn't mean I was engaged to this creature. "For luck," she said, "in finding just the right person to be your chat-friend. The rings are coded to open doors for us. But."

"But what?" I asked.

"Well," she continued, "that beard makes you look old, and hey, you *are* old for being in here. You need to be young and fresh like all people of true beauty."

I wasn't sure about this so I told her that I loved my beard, loved being a grownup adult, and that she should mind her own teenage business.

She frowned, then said, "Hey, I didn't mean you were *that* old. Or *too* old. I just meant that most people in here look better as avatars than as themselves. You should see what I really look like. I mean you *shouldn't*!" She turned her head and blushed clear through her powder and blush.

"Yes, so get an avatar please," she said, "for the sake of those who have to look at you. For *my* sake. You can be anyone you want. I can fix you up with one. It's what I do. I have great ideas and know what I like. If *I* like you, *everyone* will like you."

"I still want a beard," I said, "an even bigger one, in fact."

She seemed intrigued with this idea. Someone in the chat room actually old enough to grow his own hair.

"Hmmm," she thought for a moment. "Do you need to be human? Aha. Many of the most interesting men are not, you know. My boyfriend, for instance is a complete animal. But I'd give him up for what I'm about to make you into. Only I'm not allowed. You see, I can make men irresistible. I know a way to make you look like a king *and* keep the beard."

So she did.

~14~
The Lion and the Lady

The new lion with the fabulous mane was immediately pleased to be put in a cage with three female lions. But he soon discovered that they were more like overgrown housecats than lions. They made fun of his hair and said he was too old for them. They said his nose was too wide and the tuft of black hair at the end of his tail looked like a mouse. They also said he snored in his sleep. But he had to put up with them because the lion tamer wanted them to teach him all the tricks they knew. Every day they were herded into a big cage where they were supposed to stand on little pedestals and do demeaning things. Stupid for lions to do anyway. Actually he didn't want to do tricks at all, he just wanted to make a friend in a chat room. But now he seemed trapped. Some "king" he was turning out to be.

One day they were in the cage as usual and the lion tamer was sticking that silly chair in his face again. "One of these days," he thought, "I'm going to eat this chair, and the man holding it as well!" Then the three sissy sister cats were dismissed and he found himself alone in the cage with only a young girl, presumably for dinner. One tiny girl, one big lion. That's all. Hardly an appetizer.

The lion stepped completely down off his little pedestal and gazed at the girl cowering against the cage bars. He had never been quite so alone with a defenseless girl before and suddenly she looked somewhat familiar. There was something recognizable in her face and then he noticed that she was truly beautiful. Even to a lion. Beauty is beauty, after all. The more he stared at her, the more he became captivated by this beauty.

Soon the girl noticed his hesitation and then an element of admiration in his gaze. The admiration part was mutual, for the beast was truly magnificent. His tawny coat shimmered over his broad frame, while his muscles rippled underneath in pent-up power. His mane covered his shoulders like some splendid robe and his face radiated in regal presence.

The girl hoped the lion was not admiring her for her food value. She expected him to charge at any moment. So you can imagine her surprise when he actually started speaking to her.

"You look mouth-wateringly familiar to me," he said in a manly voice. "Have I ever attacked you before? I mean *met* you before?"

"Oh you won't do that, will you?" squealed the girl.

"Oh stop it," said the beast. "Stop crying like a frightened child. I can see by your eyes that you're not really all that frightened, and hear by your voice that you're not really a child. Are you going to faint?"

"Of course not, are you?" answered the girl, gaining courage.

"Lions don't faint," said the lion.

"I don't suppose they do," said the girl, "they just stand up on silly little pedestals and try to purr like kittens. Why are you here? Are you going to try to carry me off somewhere?"

"Of course not! Do I look like some kind of monster?"

"My tutors said that it's the beasts which turn out to be princes and the handsome princes which turn out to be beasts. I think I'd like to know what your intensions are."

"I'm not here to hurt you," said the lion.

"Well maybe then you're not really a lion," said the girl, "or you'd have eaten me by now."

"Maybe I'm not hungry."

"Maybe you're a cowardly lion."

"Don't tempt me. You're just too thin. Hardly a snack for the king of the jungle. I think maybe I'll keep you as a pet."

"Pet?" said the girl, "maybe you're a man in a cat suit. Maybe you're a boy in a cat suit. Living in this circus, I doubt you'd even know how to, say, take a girl for a walk through a real jungle."

The lion came closer with a puzzled look on his face. He nudged her gently with his nose. "Why *shouldn't* I keep you as a pet?"

"Because it's against the law of the jungle," she said.

"What law of the jungle?" he asked.

"The one posted right over there on the wall," she said.

The Law of the Jungle

1. Eat or be eaten
2. Follow your leader
3. If you can't fight, run
4. If you can't run, fight
5. If you can't run or fight, play dead
6. If you can't do any of these things, taste very bad
7. Honor the opposite sex
8. Train up the young, then kick them out
9. Love El for He created you, honor Man for he has dominion over you.
10. Poop only in long grass

"You see," the girl continued, "you have to honor me. So could you please honor my wishes and take me for a short walk in your jungle? Then bring me right back here?"

The lion seemed confused.

"I'm not going to ask twice," she said.

"Well, maybe I'll just try that," he replied.

"Try?" she said, "Are you unsure of your capabilities as a lion to take a lady for a walk in the jungle?"

"There's no jungle around here," he admitted, "and what's more, I was born in a small zoo near a shopping mall. Not Africa. So you see I can't take you to the jungle, but if it wasn't for this cage, I could chase you all around this house. Would that be fun?"

The girl looked deep into his eyes and then slowly put her hands to her mouth.

"There once was a lion from the stores," she said through her fingers.
"Who chased a poor girl through the floors;
In circles they went,
Until he was spent,
And ended up leaving on all fours."

"Does that remind you of anything?" she asked.

Now a male lion has a big head but a rather small brain, at least when it comes to remembering things that happened with girls more than thirty years ago. But slowly it dawned on him that the girl he was about to eat was someone he knew, someone he admired but who had never admired him back. Yet here she was, doing plenty of admiring now – now that he was a lion.

"Mary? Is that you? You don't look like yourself."

"Look whose talking," said the girl. "William, I don't recall you having quite so much hair."

"Mary! May I hug you?"

"Not a chance, beast," said Mary. "But if you hold very still I'll come up and hug you."

So the lion, who was me by the way, held very still while Mary slid up to him and buried her arms in his mane. My mane, that is. I closed my eyes and would have purred if I had been a purring cat. Well maybe I did purr, but don't tell anybody.

Then suddenly and in one single motion she grabbed my neck and swung her right leg over my back. I jumped up but she was already fully astride with her chin resting between my ears. So what could I do but give Mary a merry ride all around the cage. I had to, it was part of the Law of the Jungle.

~15~
Getting Out

It is all well and good to prance around a cage with a beautiful girl on your back, but what would happen when the lion tamer returned to find out that I had not eaten my supper. He hated it when I played with my food. He told me that growing up on the farm, they never gave names to animals they were going to eat. And they never kept them as pets or fell in love with them. Now I was guilty of all three, especially the falling in love part.

Mary was truly delightful and very brave as she guided me around the ring with her legs and heals. Sometimes she'd even pull my ears. Then she'd yell "mush, haw, gee" or "whoa" as if commanding a dog. Sure, I loved her, but I was a beast nevertheless and didn't even trust myself. One reckless snap of my teeth and she'd be mush herself.

Just for fun she covered my eyes with her dainty hands, but I shook my main vigorously, throwing her ingloriously onto the sawdust floor. "Oh, I'm so sorry,"

I said, trying to lick her cheek. But my tongue was so big it got her lips, nose and eyes as well, which made her frown at me.

"But I suppose it's not your fault," she said, brushing herself off, "I was blinding you. I must have scared you."

"Nothing scares a lion," I said, trying to flaunt my mane into her face.

"Hair doesn't make a man," she said. "Besides, I have longer hair than you."

"I'm a lion, not a man," I said.

She laughed. "You're only an avatar of poor William who got stuck in a dollhouse."

"Look who's talking," I said.

"Okay," she said, "I'll call you William the Lion King of Scotland. But captive in a French château."

"By the way, how do we get out of here?" I asked.

Mary winced. "Well, if I try real hard, yes, if I squeeze. Ouch. Oh. Oops. Stop staring. Maybe if I hold my breath. There, see, I'm through. I'm through the bars and out of the cage. Good thing my avatar is so slim and stylish." She cocked her head and waved at me from outside the bars.

"You're not leaving me in here, are you?" I said.

"Beasts belong in cages," she said.

"But I'm not a beast, I'm your Willy!"

"Oh I suppose so, of course." She laughed. "I was just kidding. You're my pet lion and I'll take care of you, don't worry. Only I don't quite know how to at the moment. And my arm is quite numb. Is it from riding you, or squeezing through the bars? Or?"

Just then I had a bright idea. "When I got my ring, the girl said it would unlock doors for me. Why don't you try yours."

"How?" she replied, "I never heard of rings unlocking doors."

"What, you never heard of a key ring?" I said, but she didn't think it was funny. "Just hold your ring up to the padlock and see what happens."

So she tried to take the ring off but her finger was too swollen and numb. Her whole arm in fact.

So she held her whole hand up to the lock and the smiley face stone in the ring gladly jumped out and into the keyhole of the lock. "I love unlocking locks," he said.

Sure enough the padlock unlocked instantly, but Mary noticed something else happening. The numbness and swelling was leaving her arm and fingers. "I wonder if that smiley face Mister Vick Cyrus has anything to do with this?" she pondered. When she noticed her lion wearing a similar ring on his left front paw, and saw that he was limping on it a bit, she became sure.

"Willy," she said, opening the cage door quickly, "run out of there now and let me up on your back." This I did and we sped off before Vick Cyrus could get out of the lock and back onto her finger.

"Way hate," Cyrus cried, "you more-got fee! Get hack beer!"

But it was too late, we were well outside the circus room and heading for – well, we didn't exactly know where we were heading. Mary made me throw away my ring as well. So with no ring to guide us, we were just running a Mary chase, Willy-nilly. I mean I was running; she was riding. And doing most of the driving, I might add.

~16~
Shutting Down

A Mary chase it was, Willy-nilly into this and that private alcove, this and that chat room, this and that – oh my goodness, you should have seen people's faces at the sight of a girl on a lion barging through their discussions or tennis matches or candlelight dinners. One time we knocked over a Grecian urn full of – well, grease of course. That made us skate headlong through a curtain and into the Pigwarts School of Witchardry. That place gave me the willies, but Mary just laughed and dug her heels deeper into my sides.

Another time we entered a movie set, scared some horses away and made the cute little girl cry. There is always a cute little girl in horse movies. In the film she was supposed to rescue horses from rustlers. Without the horses to rustle the rustlers kidnapped the girl instead. So we gave chase. Now a lion can never outrun a horse, but that day I did. Just to impress Mary I suppose. Saving a cute little girl was also some motivation. Of course, when we were talking with her afterwards we discovered she was just the avatar of an ugly, pimple-faced fifteen year old playing in her room. She did this every day after school 'till her mom got home. Later I told Mary that I didn't believe there could be such a thing as an ugly fifteen year old. Eventually I found this to be true, because seeing through God's eyes is like putting on truth glasses which never fog up or lose focus. "People judge by outward appearance, but the LORD looks at the heart." says 1 Samuel 16:7.

And that day I had a lion heart. So Mary spurred me on and on. One minute we were in Narnia, the next Middle Earth, then Oz, Tatooine, Gotham. It was all becoming a blur, but Mary was loving it. And then, to cap it off, Spiderman hung down upside down and actually tried to kiss her. There I put my foot down. Actually I put four of them down and we sped off.

"Hey cat-man," Mary yelled in my ear, "you're not getting jealous are you? Let's go see if we can find Tarzan again. I'd like to see the expression on his face when he sees what I've got."

A Mary chase it was, Willy-nilly until we realized we were actually getting nowhere. In reality we were just two people sitting at two different computers connected to the same cyber world. It was all fantasy, folly and fruitless.

"Hey," said Mary, "we'll never get out of here this way. Why don't you just log off and come over here and rescue me in person. Where are you anyway?"

"To tell you the truth," I said, "I'm just downstairs. I own Aunt Clara's house, remember?"

Mary couldn't remember if she was supposed to remember that or not, so she just told me to shut up, shut down my computer and get up to the third floor as soon as possible. That, as I remembered was more easily said than done. But I told her I would try. First I hid her in a closet of costumes, way in the back with the animal skins. She insisted on putting on a leopard outfit and what could I say, dressed as a lion and everything. Then I turned off my computer and we disappeared to each other. I headed up the stairs and she snuggled up against a black panther coat.

~17~
Getting In

Actually I bounded up the stairs like a lion. Of course I was not a lion, just a nifty fifty year old man who nevertheless had to stop and rest at the top of every flight. But please don't tell Mary that. I wanted to be her lion king so bad. But in the end it didn't exactly work out that way. Now no fair skipping to the back of the book. Let me tell this story in my own way, okay. Do we have a deal?

So I had not the faintest idea how to find Mary, or even how to enter a dollhouse again. That became plainly evident when I couldn't even get through the front door of Mousumerset Manor. Yes, I tried every window and even the chimney. Yes, *all* the chimneys. Nothing worked.

Then I saw the June-bug. It was prancing around on five legs in the general direction of the house.

"Hello, Mister man. Don'tcha love it the way I can march on five legs? My name's April. I'm here to see the Mayfly," said the June-bug. "I lost a leg to a whale of a big stag beetle back in July. So you can't get into this august house, huh? Poor thing. Haven't ya even read your own books? Don'tcha think you'll need that magic sword to get in? The one in the castle? And I'd also go back and fetch your Bible. You'll need it. I always have mine. The only good ones inside are in spider slang-uage. But most non-spiders find reading them to be rather sticky going. The grasshopper versions are changed liberally every year to match modern attitudes. And the ants don't have Bibles at all, only books on how to be more sociable. Roaches, as everyone knows, can't read. But we beetles have good Bibles, don'tcha love it?"

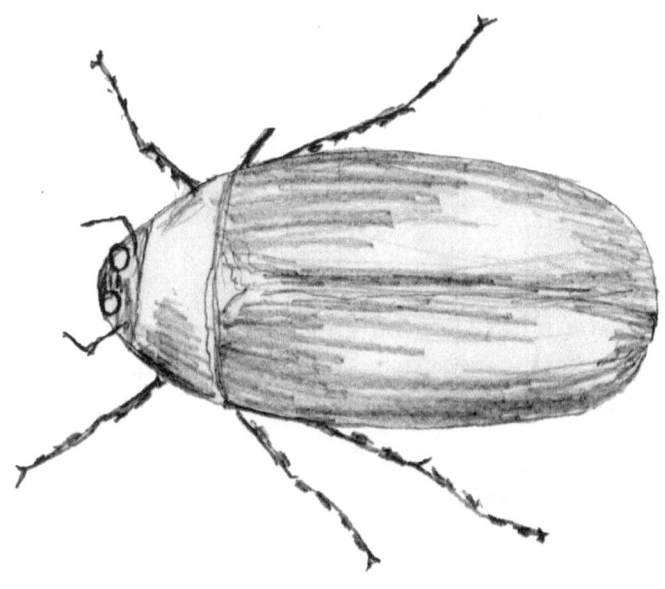

I thanked the June-bug profusely, shook three of his five hands and sped downstairs to retrieve my Bible. I had not meant to be here without it. But it was not where I usually keep it beside my bed. I was beside myself, and besides, it's not like me to misplace things. I finally found it in my car and remembered I hadn't used it since last Sunday at church! I guess as a lion I didn't have much interest in the Bible. Silly of course because there are lots of lions in it. My favorite is the Lion of Judah, my personal hero.

So, with Bible in hand, I approached the imposing Castle Levancrieff. Of course, it was imposing only to rats because it was after all just a dollhouse. Yet it had many stone towers, slate roofs, and great iron grates everywhere. It had a thick wooden drawbridge across a watery moat with real snakes in it. Everything a man could want. Still I had no idea how I would get in, or how I would get the sword *out*. So there I was, pulling the tiny chain that served as a doorbell. Presently a small rat nose appeared through a knothole in the drawbridge.

"May I come in?" I asked.

"We don't like giants," said the rat timidly, mostly through his nostrils. "Besides, you wouldn't *fit* in."

Then the rat put his bulging, black eye to the hole and spied my Bible. "Is that a magic book?" he asked.

"No, it's a Bible," I said.

"Aha, thought so," said the rat. "I can use it to get you in, if you'll promise to give me a blessing when I do."

"What kind of blessing?"

"That's up to you, giant, but if I don't like it, I'm kicking you out again."

"That sounds fair," I said. "Okay, get me in."

The rat motioned me to hold the Bible up to the door.

"Abracadabra," he snorted, mostly through his nose. "Read and look. Mark 10:25 to 27, in the Book. Eye of camel, see the way; eye of needle, you're in today!"

With this, he beckoned me in and sure enough I was able to shrink enough to fit nicely though the opening gate. "See," he said, "your bible is full of magic. Now give me my blessing. Remember I have to like it or out you go again."

"To begin with, kind Mister Rat…:

"My name is Ratfink," he interrupted.

"Okay Ratfink," I said, "first of all my Bible bears no magic as you say. That power comes from somewhere else. Somewhere in dirty, dark corners and deceitful hiding places. But neither does my Bible bear malice toward you. In fact here is a nice blessing for you and all ratdom.

"'Leviticus 11:29. Of the small animals that scurry along the ground, these are unclean for you: the mole rat, the rat, large lizards of all kinds.'"

"What!" said the rat. "Unclean! Not! We are constantly bathing, unlike humans. We can smell you from a mile away." With this the rat raised his sword to drive me out of the castle.

"Wait," I cried, "unclean only means we're not allowed to eat you. So you're a protected species. That's good. That's the blessing. Don't you like it?"

"Well it's a mixed blessing at best," said the rat. "I'd rather be thought of as clean. I just licked myself this morning. Okay mole rats are dirty because they dig in the ground so much and lizards are dirty because their tongues are too thin to wash themselves properly. So I suppose you can stay, since you won't be eating any of us. You must understand, however, that we have no such prohibitions against eating *you*!"

"I'll take my chances," I said, clutching my Bible. "Where is Prince Sherwoode? Could you summon him for me?"

"Don't be silly," said the rat, "no one *summons* the prince. He's way too important for that. Besides he sleeps all the time. He never hears us."

"Then I'll just go and find him myself," I said. And I did.

~18~
The Prince & the Princess

It was a long way to the top of the tower where the prince slept. I had to ask directions several times from ants who never lie, from grasshoppers who never tell the truth, and from roaches who never quite get the point of your question. Finally, after all this, I woke the sleeping prince by tickling his whiskers with his tail.

"Prince Sherwood," I said, "My name is William."

"Yes, I figured as much, I'll just call you Willykins for short. You can call me Woodiekins for short."

"But Woodiekins isn't shorter than Sherwood," I said.

"That's what your sister said," said Woodiekins, "but everyone keeps using it anyway. So there! It must be shorter. So why are you here, Willykins?"

"I would like to borrow the greatsword Logokrataioo," I said.

"Well, well," said the rat, "seems to me you humans don't understand the full definition of the word 'borrow.' It means to take *with permission* and bring *back* as well. Anything else, we rats tend to call 'stealing.'"

"Oh, I know," I said. "My sister didn't mean to steal anything. She just forgot to return it. I have a better memory than she."

"Well anyway, that doesn't matter" said the rat. "I don't have the sword. My father has it and he's out on another crusade. He has an army that goes around wearing crosses and killing non-Christians. That way he gets them to become Christians. The ones he doesn't kill that is. Doesn't make a whole lot of sense to me. What's the point of being a Christian anyway? You aren't one, are you?"

"I'm born again," I said, "if that's what you mean."

"Born again?" blurted the rat. "Disgusting. It was gross enough the first time, and I was much smaller then."

"I'm talking about rebirth as a new creature with the Holy Spirit coming to live inside you," I said.

"Oh that," said Woodiekins, "I've heard of that, but it's only for humans. You're lucky. We rats just have El. We only play at being Christians. We don't really know God like you do."

"Not all of us humans know Him," I said. "Some of us purposefully reject him."

"Oh really," said the rat. "How awful. Let's send my father to put the sword into them."

"That's not helpful," I said, "God has special plans for them – their lot will be a lot worse than that."

"Well good for him," said Woodiekins, "sorry I can't lend you the sword. You'll need more magic than a

90

Ratfink spell to get into Mousumerset Manor. You'll need the power of the sword for sure."

Just then I remembered something. I had a sword right there with me. A great two-edged sword right under my arm.

"Hey Woodiekins," I said, "look at this. Hebrews 4:12 [NIV] says: 'For the word of God is living and active. Sharper than any double-edged sword, it penetrates ...'"

"How does a book penetrate?" interrupted Woodiekins.

I continued reading from the book. "Luke 11:10 says: 'For everyone who asks, receives. Everyone who seeks, finds. And to everyone who knocks, the door will be opened.' Hey, that must mean I can go anywhere I want, if I claim the promise in this verse."

"Why don't you try it and see if it works!" said Woodiekins.

So I did.

At first I thought it was a failure because I couldn't even find my way out of the castle. I came upon many a locked door and most of them wouldn't open even if I placed my right hand on the Bible and added 'abracadabra' to my prayers. But some did.

Finally I came upon a particularly thick door with a rounded top and more than several locks on it. It had a tiny window in the middle which I opened just out of curiosity. There inside, fast asleep on a pile of straw was the most beautiful girl I had ever seen. A *human* girl. She had long blond hair, a thin waist and wonderfully delicate arms. I couldn't see her face for it was buried in the hay.

"Hey!" I called out, but there was no response. Maybe she was dead, but her skin was too pleasingly pink for that. "Pssst," I tried again. I didn't want to make too much noise because clearly she was a prisoner here. But why? Was she a slave? A runaway teenager? A captive fairy who'd lost her wings over the years? My mind was racing.

Just then all the heavy locks on the door fell open all by themselves. It was kind of like a miracle. I mean she was a miracle all by herself and then the locks just opened all by themselves. Miracle enough to make my knees wobble, you can believe. So timidly I walked in. There was a plate of half eaten bread by her head and under her arm was a magic wand of sorts.

Now to waken a rat you just tickle its whiskers with its tail. But this lovely creature had neither. Neither can you just grab her, or even touch her. She was like fine china, and her fingers were of fragile crystal. I touched one anyway and she tucked her hand under her waist. Well at least she wasn't dead.

I bent down protectively over her. "Are you sleeping?" I whispered gently in her ear. At this, she jerked, turned her head quickly and tried to rise, bumping me in the nose as she did.

"Well I suppose that will have to do," she said.

"Do for what?" I asked.

"For a kiss," she said, and gazed down into the straw. "My name is Sleeping Cutie and I'm supposed to marry the first handsome prince who kisses me. Lucky you, I guess. And lucky me that rat princes don't count."

I just stood there stupidly.

"Well I guess you're not half bad after all," she continued, slowly looking up. "The beard threw me off at first. But it's growing on me. I kinda like it even. Oh, I mean it's growing on *you*! You must be at least thirty!" Her tiny laugh was enticing – soothing as a dove, innocent as a sparrow.

Just then she thought of something and covered her face with her hands.

"What's wrong," I asked.

"You *are* a prince, aren't you?" Her eyes were pleading through her fingers. "Oh please say yes. Please."

She put her hands down and gazed into my eyes. I thought for a moment and then made the mistake of gazing back. And that was the end of it. I'd fallen into her spell and the middle of my chest began to ache with love, I'm embarrassed to say.

"I'll be your prince forever," I bleated from my pounding heart. "But come on, we need to escape *now* from this castle. Hurry up. Gather your things."

"I only have this wand," she said. "Without it I lose my good looks, so they let me keep it. Do you want me to use it on you?"

"Oh stop it!" I said. "Hurry up. Don't you have any shoes?"

"No, are they necessary?" she said. "I'm a princess. I never go outside."

"Well I guess not," I said, looking at her fair skin and gentle features. "But come – never mind your hair, it looks just fine." She was gorgeous, but like a child and a princess combined, she was already becoming a handful, as you can imagine.

"What's your name?" she asked me in a sweet voice.

"William. No – Willy," I replied, "what's yours?"

"No," she answered, "I'll call you Will. Because you will. I *know* you will."

"Will what?" I asked.

"Will say 'I will,'" she said. "And you may call me Mari. Pronounce it 'Marry,' okay?"

"Yes, ok Mari," I said. "Come and don't forget your wand."

As it turned out her wand would create many more problems than it would solve.

~19~
Escaping the Castle

My Bible was able to unlock several doors and soon my princess and I were hand in hand, down to the ground floor of the castle and nearly to the drawbridge. I was beginning to think it was God opening and shutting doors for us and not any magic in my Bible. Mari agreed. She said Bibles aren't supposed to be magic books. I'm sure she's right.

My new companion was remarkably fast on her bare feet and it was I who made all the noise in my hiking boots. Well, don't laugh, I didn't know how far this adventure would take me. So I wore my boots, okay?

We were almost out of the castle and home free when my girl said to me, "I need to go down there." She pointed our joined hands to a small wall-opening leading to a dark, spiral staircase. It was roughly carved through the solid rock foundation and looked like a hungry mouth.

"What's down there?" I enquired.

"Where my wand came from," she said. "I have one piece of unfinished business down there."

But just then no less than the entire rat crusade army came marching across the drawbridge and into the castle. There were thousands of them, arranged in orderly rows and carrying Christian flags. How ironic because, like most crusaders of old (and even some modern ones), they weren't Christians at all, but simply rats. They stomped their feet as they marched, which made quite a noise because a rat army has twice as many feet as a human one. Poor Mari and I barely had a chance to scurry under the base of the drawbridge before they came.

"So are you a princess?" I asked. I had to talk directly into her ear, the din was so loud.

"Of course," she said. Her lips and nose brushed the edge of my hair as she talked.

"How exciting," I said, "is it hard work being a princess?"

"Not at all," she replied, "we princesses have a strict code to live by. That makes it easy. Here it is:

The Little Royal Princess's Strict Code of Stately Conduct

1. Be the youngest daughter in your family
2. If you're not the youngest, be the cutest
3. Eat only what you want
4. Sleep only when you want
5. Wear anything you want
6. Play with anything you want
7. Yell at anyone you want
8. Hit anyone you want
9. Marry anyone you want

I tried to frown at her because I thought her code was more like a code for spoiled brats. But my frown turned limp on my lips in the face of her soul crushing sweetness.

"Why don't we just swim for it!" I said finally.

"I need to finish my business," she said. "Besides there're snakes in the moat."

"What's your business in there, anyway?" I demanded. "We're free now aren't we?"

"Maybe *you* are," she replied, "but first I've got a score to settle. Are you with me, my love, my Will?"

"Sure," I said protectively. I felt completely captive by her charms, but not trapped. I was staying of my own free will. She looked so reassured and sweeter than ever. Right there under the bridge of marching rat boots we embraced and time began to stand still.

Actually it didn't. It flew by and suddenly there was no rat army anymore. They were all inside drinking ginger beer. She grabbed my hand again and led me back into the hall – down the mysterious mouth leading deep into the rock. We had to go single file. I placed my hand on her shoulder because it was getting dark, and then completely black. The farther down we got, the colder we became until finally at the bottom we had to bundle together arm in arm. Slowly we inched along a rough rock wall until she found another opening.

"Oh please, no more stairs," I pleaded, but she shushed me and squeezed my arm reassuringly.

The opening was in fact a long hall and there, at the end was a flickering fire. Toward it we crept, silent as mice.

About halfway we encountered another staircase but she avoided it carefully.

"Down there I got my wand," she said. "Don't ever go there! Even in your mind."

Presently we came into a small cavern with a round, open fireplace in the middle. It afforded light, heat and kept some of the dank air at bay. I could only imagine what other creatures it might be keeping away. The room was filled with intricate instruments and menacing machines.

"Good, no guards," she said. "They must be up celebrating the return of the army."

"Were you in here before?" I whispered, as the full horror of it began to dawn on me. The room was full of instruments of torture. In one corner was an interrogation chair with sharp spikes all over it. In another was a garrote, a chair with a tall pole as a back. On the pole was a leather strap to hold the head in position as a sharpened screw bored into the back of the neck. In the center of the room near the fire was a table called the 'rack.' It was used to stretch a person. Off to one side was an 'iron maiden,' a coffin-shaped box with two doors which accessed an interior studded with spikes.

I stared in horror at Mari, "You weren't…"

"Yes." Her voice began to tremble. "I was sent here by my father to be the wife of the rat king. My father said if I did this the rats would not attack our country.

But once I arrived the rat king said I was too homely and sent me down here to die. They kept me in that cage hanging over there and fed me what the other prisoners wouldn't eat. One day during cleaning I escaped and ran down those stairs we just passed. Two guards gave chase but they never returned from that death hole. There I found my wand. It saved me. Don't ever ask me about it again.

"See these tongs?" she continued. "They use them to threaten people with hot coals."

She picked one up and waved it in my face. "Coals like this," she said. I could feel the heat on my face and the fear in my heart. But instead of replacing it in the fire she set it on the wooden torture chair. Then she put another on the wooden torture rack, then another on a bale of straw by the woodpile.

"I think we can leave now," she said and I quite agreed. But first she picked up a large metal bucket and filled it to the brim with the rest of the live coals. This she threw down the dreaded death hole as we ran past.

As we were flying up the stairs we heard a muffled explosion. Then another. Then we were out the door and almost free of the castle when the imposing figure of Ratfink blocked our way over the drawbridge.

"Aha," he said. "A human being naughty again. Stealing yet. And stealing another human, no less. Hand over the girl, she's mine."

"That I can't do," I said. "we're engaged."

"We don't recognize that sort of stuff here," he said. "We're not stingy like humans. We share. So hand her over."

I raised my hand in protest, but Ratfink raised his sword. Just as I was about to back down Mari raised her wand and gave it just the slightest little flick toward the rat. Instantly he was transformed into what can only be described as a rat dude. A rat dude with muscles, a big chest, slim hips and a very curvaceous tail. His whiskers became longer, his face broader and his eyes bulgier. Even his teeth were even. Whiter too. His coat became splendidly shiny as was his nose. All very pleasing – to a rat that is.

The immediate effect was that Ratfink couldn't take his eyes off himself. While he was admiring his face in his metal shield, Mari and I slipped by and out onto the drawbridge. There she did the same wand thing to several large snakes which then became quite taken with their reflections in the water. So we made our escape and immediately grew to normal human size.

"Mari," I asked later, as we were sitting downstairs to dinner at my dining room table. "Are you in love with your looks as much as those snakes were?"

She self-consciously touched her wand to her forehead and said, "I was at first – and that's why I tried to sleep all the time. It's never good to be overly or overtly in love with your looks. But then my handsome prince came, kissed me, and now that's all transferred over to him. Right, my love, my Will?"

I had to admit that it was, but I didn't admit it to her. At least not with my mouth, but I knew she could see it in my eyes.

"So where are you going to carry me off to, my love, my Will?" she asked shyly. I thought about it, but somehow I feared we'd end up going wherever she wanted.

"Well," I said, "First I'm on my way up to rescue my Mary from that mansion on the third floor?"

"Your Mary?" she looked shocked and hurt. "Who's *she*, and what about your Mari?"

"Oh Mary," I said, "she's just a lion tamer who can actually ride her lions. A family friend. But you're my Mari who has tamed me and will marry me."

She smiled and gave me a kiss on the cheek. I didn't mind that one bit. When she buried her hand in my hair I almost purred. Well I suppose I *did*.

~20~
Interlude in Real Life

It was Saturday and I put Mari to bed in the guest bedroom. That's where I used to sleep before Aunt Clara died. Mari was no trouble at all because she didn't have any extra clothes – nothing at all except what she was wearing and of course, her wand. She kept joking about using it on me, but I told her she shouldn't or I'd have to get another driver's license picture. They'd ask questions about how I'd become so handsome all of a sudden.

Luckily I found some of Katherine's old clothes in a closet. We picked out a nightgown and a nice church dress for tomorrow. We also picked out a story we found in the Bible. Tomorrow at church we'd say she was my sister Sarah from Cincinnati. It's true, look it up in Genesis 20:2.

Mari wanted to immediately pretend we were already married but I insisted we wait until we were in fact *already* married. She seemed confused but I told her I'd explain when we saw each other again at breakfast. She asked if there were any eggs in the house but I told her I ate only Cheerios. She didn't know what they were but seemed willing to "try one or two." In the morning she ended up eating six-hundred and twelve.

I asked if she wanted to pray before going to sleep. She thought I said 'play' and threw a pillow at me.

"No, *pray*," I said, "talk to God."

"Why ever for?" she asked. "Besides I don't know any prayers. Why don't you say one for me."

Somehow I thought her eyes were laughing at me so I told her to forget it and retreated into my own room.

At church the next day she asked me if we could go ahead and get married right then. I said I was willing, and I really was, but I whispered to her that this particular church wouldn't let a person marry his sister.

"Oh that's right," she said, "oh well, we'll just have to go to the town hall."

"Not open on Sundays," I said.

"This sucks," she said, "when you're in love, your church rules just get in the way. Besides church rules only make you look good on the outside. In our hearts we're already married." Her long fingernails dug into my arm.

"Anyway, who needs a silly ceremony to tell us when we're married!" she cried.

"I do," I said, "I do before I say 'I do.'"

"Then say 'I will,'" she said, "say 'I will marry you,' because your name is Will and mine is Mari. I Will Mari you."

I laughed and kissed her right there in the pew. I hoped nobody saw us, for the church frowns on kissing in church. Especially if she's your sister. Or maybe I was glad they saw us, or even recognized that she was not my sister. You see, I was so proud to have her with me and to show her off. What a prize she was.

Nobody spoke to us as we left the church but I noticed many heads turning in our direction. No one could keep their gaze off of her. She received the stare of an eye as a cat receives the stroke of a hand.

On the drive home she fell asleep against my shoulder and I was alone with my thoughts. I really did love her. I couldn't help loving her. But was I being trapped by her love? I added up the reasons I was sure God had brought her to me.

How a Man Knows God is Bringing a Particular Woman to Him

1. She is beautiful
2. He feels so good when he is with her
3. She is attractive
4. She never lies to him
5. She is gorgeous
6. It's such a coincidence that they met at all
7. She is stunning
8. She always wants to hold hands and kiss
9. She is dazzling
10. Her daddy is probably rich

On the other side of the coin there were only two things still eating at my mind.

1. What about Mary, who I had left waiting for me in a leopard costume and sleeping on a black panther coat.

2. What happens if Mari loses that wand of hers?

Shortly after we got home Mari waylaid me in the hall on my way to fix lunch. She had found an old sundress of Katherine's and it looked very nice on her.

She grabbed the front of my shirt in her fists. "I don't know if I can wait till tomorrow to get married," she said.

"It's Sunday," I said, kind of in a rush to get the hamburgers on.

"Why can't we do it ourselves today," she said, "and sign the papers tomorrow?"

"Because the Bible says the papers come first," I insisted, although my heart said otherwise.

She looked hurt.

"And another thing," I said, "I really need to go into the mansion right after lunch. Will you come with me, or not?"

She looked shocked.

"Well?" I stared right into her big eyes.

She didn't back down or look away. "You said you would marry me, my love, my Will." she said.

"Then come into the mansion with me," I said. "I need to rescue Mary first."

"In that case," she said, "I guess I better had."

We kissed and that was that. "You like hamburgers, don't you," I said.

"Cheeseburgers too," she said, "rare with relish."

~21~
The Most Beautiful Mouse

Mari and I stood before the impressive door of Mousumerset Manor. I carried my Bible and she had her wand. With it she tapped on the door. I had no idea if we'd be able to shrink enough to enter.

Soon the door opened and I recognized Luucy, who was bubbly and bothersome as usual.

"It's not polite to rap on a door with a stick," said Luucy in a thin voice. "But you may have a warm crumpet anyway. Come in. Oh hello William, you may have two, since you're a man."

So we had no trouble shrinking this time, which was nice because crumpets become a great deal bigger when you're a great deal smaller. After we had finished eating (Mari had seconds by the way), Luucy asked what our business was in the Manor.

"We're going to get married," said Mari immediately.

"Oh my," replied Luucy, "Have you made out the guest list, ordered your cake, your wedding dress?

Where's your ring? Haven't you seen our checklist for brides?"

"No," said Mari, "we're not having a cake or a dress, not even a checklist."

"What no dress?" cried Luucy. "Strapless is in. You're the first girl I've seen who could carry that off to advantage. Of course mice have the advantage here because they don't walk upright. What a shame to miss out on strapless! And think of the pictures you won't be able to give your children!"

"We're not having children," said Mari. "We'll be too busy making each other blissful."

I shot Mari a glance and said, "Luucy, we really came to see the bat."

"He's going to marry us, "said Mari.

I finally had to grab Mari's hand. "Yes, after we come out of the Château."

"Oh, you mean Château Etiquette?" said Luucy. "You should get married in there. No one does it better than the French."

"Yes, whatever," I said. "But we must get going, Luucy. Time is urgent."

"Yes," said the mouse, motioning toward the door. "It always is for engaged couples. Enjoy your stay then. And congratulations William."

"Thank you," said Mari, grinning broadly.

On the way up the stairs we met Adeylia. Now, as Mari is the most beautiful girl on the block, Adeylia is the most beautiful mouse in the house. That includes hamsters too. If I described her to you, you'd just say, "Oh that's just a mouse," but to mice, well they know the difference between just being female and being fantastic.

Like I said, we met on the way up. Adeylia, the self-proclaimed prima donna of politeness engaged me in courteous conversation, all the while ignoring Mari standing below me on the stairs at my back.

"Finally I meet a real man with facial hair," said Adeylia, twitching her tiny nose. "Does it itch?"

"Not a bit," I said, "it's surprisingly soft to the touch."

"May I try," asked the mouse.

"Oh sorry," interjected Mari, pushing me steadily in the back with her wand. "We're headed upstairs for our wedding. And by the way, the beard belongs to me."

"Oh really?" countered Adeylia, "are you the 'bearded lady?'"

"No, that distinction belongs to you, fuzzy face," said Mari.

Adeylia gave her a stare with her big, black, bulging eyes but Mari shot right back with her baby blues. "Let us pass," she said, "or I'll put a spell on you with my wand."

"What kind of a spell?" Adeylia cocked her ears.

"It makes you irresistibly beautiful," said Mari.

"Didn't quite work on *you*, did it?" said Adeylia.

With this Mari flicked her wand at the mouse and presto – nothing happened. She shook it again – and nothing.

"See! It doesn't work on me either," said Adeylia. "You see, I'm already the world's most beautiful."

"Well we can easily fix that with a fist!" said Mari.

Here I felt compelled to step in and pulled Mari's arm past the mouse and clear up the stairs.

"The nerve of that rodent," she said. "Don't you just hate their ugly tails? Don't you just hate the way they wiggle their noses at you and twiddle their whiskers. Don't you just hate their mousy-brown hair? Don't you just..."

"Come on, Mari," I said, "just leave her behind. We need to find our way up to the bat's chambers."

"Oh yeah, chambers, to get married," she said.

"Yeah, as soon we come out of Château Libéré.

~22~
The Most Beautiful Bug

In our haste to get away from Adeylia, Mari and I got lost again. I think she was getting tired of all this endless walking through halls, corridors and passageways. When we got to the fainting sofa she just wanted to lie down and take a nap. She wanted me to lie down too, but there wasn't room. While she slept I paced the hall and reminisced about how Mary had kidded me years ago about this very fainting sofa. "A fainting sofa is always essential for graceful reclining in a formal setting," she had said. We were young then, but I remember exactly how she looked, wearing a modest yellow sun dress, with her hair nicely brushed back into a ponytail. Perhaps we were in love. More likely we didn't even know what love was. I gazed back at the amazing creature on the sofa. Now *that* was real love.

Eventually she awoke and we continued our journey, hand in hand. It was not long before we reached a semi-dark chamber with pictures all over the walls. They were hanging all the way up to the ceiling and all the way down to the floor. I had a sneaky suspicion about that room but I didn't want to alarm Mari. When I spied black legs darting in and out from behind the frames, I held Mari close and whispered in her ear.

"Don't be afraid, honey," I said quietly, "I'm here."

"I'm here too," she said, "that's why I'm afraid. But I have my wand," she added.

Sure enough, before we were halfway across the floor a black apparition slid slowly down a silk strand and into our faces.

"Sintruders!" it said in a syrupy sweet voice. "Sinvaders! Scum to sock-you-pie sour space. Sleeve! Sexit!"

"Sold on," I said in my best spiderese, "I'm on my sway to rescue Smary. Stew you snow Smary?"

"Swee stew. Swee stew!" said the spider, "swear siz she? Syme her best friendly friendie. Syme Shcandelaria!"

"Never mind that," said Mari. "Just let us pass, you ugly thing."

"Swell, you scan pass anything you want," said Shcandelaria, "only don't be rude about it." The spider was trying to mimic Mari's accent but not doing too well.

"Then get out of our way before I hit you with this stick," warned Mari.

"Sticks and stones may strike our heads but silly threats we never dreads," replied the spider, bobbing up and down in front of Mari's face.

"It's a magic wand!" said Mari.

"Won't stew a spit of good!" spit the brave spider back into her face.

"Mari," I said, "I think we should just leave."

"Not until I teach this bug a lesson," said Mari.

With that she shook her wand vigorously at Shcandelaria and when nothing happened she flapped it at her repeatedly like a drum stick. This time something did happen – but it was most unexpected. Whatever the wand was doing to the spider just seemed to bounce off, right back into the wand itself. It started to get hot in Mari's hand. Then it began to disintegrate. Slowly at first, but eventually it flaked and crumbled away right through her fingers. In less than a minute it was nothing but dust at her feet.

"Aha," said Shcandelaria, "I break scameras stew! Nothing scan make a spider beautiful. Nothing. Many of us die trying, but most spiders just learn to accept themselves as they are. And that's what you should stew, Miss Plain Jane!"

Mari and I ran directly out of there and straight into the bat's chambers. As our eyes adjusted to the light I noticed that Mari had changed. Her long, flowing blond hair had become, well lets say more scraggly than flowing and more like dishwater than blond. Her big blue eyes were now gray and dull. Her beautiful, full mouth had become thin lipped and small. Her cute, up turned nose had become rather too large and hung on her face like a muzzle. Her clear skin was suddenly scarred and her figure, which had been the apple of my eye, was now more like – well, an apple itself.

"Oh my wand is gone!" she sobbed and looked up into my horrified face. "Oh Will! What *will* I do? What will *you* do?" She just wept and wept.

Then the most amazing thing in this book happened. I looked down into her tortured and tear-stained face, brushed some untamed hair out of her eyes, then took her bruised body into my arms and said, "Oh Mari, I know very well what I'm going to do. I'm going to *marry* you!"

~23~
We Finally See the Bat

In our preoccupation with each other we lost sight of the fact that we were actually in the bat's chambers. We were wiping away each other's tears when we heard a distinct rustle of wings and then a clearing of throat.

"A touching love scene," came the voice, "but a tangled and dangerous web of emotions, nevertheless."

We had no idea what the bat was saying to us, or even if he was dangerous, really a vampire, or something worse. So I stepped protectively in front of my girl and uttered the most pertinent and scholarly remark I could think of.

"Huh?" I said.

"Apologies," said the bat, "to wake you from your dream. No, that would be your daydream. No, in fact that would be your dream world. Your reverie. Your rendezvous. Your tryst."

"Huh?" we both said together.

"Oh, but that's your affair entirely," said the bat, "but how now does it concern me, as evidenced by your presence here?"

"We want you to marry us right now – immediately," I stammered.

"Oh," said the bat, "from the looks of it you're already married."

"I assure you we're *not*," I said.

"Then well and good," said the bat, "clear heads have prevailed. Young lady is it your intension to have this much older man?"

"It is," said Mari, "even though he now knows I'm not worthy of him."

"Why aren't you worthy of him?" asked the bat.

"Because I'm plain and scarred."

"I see," said the bat. "An interesting reason. And you sir, is it your intension to have this plain and scarred little girl?"

"She's not little," I said, "and my heart reaches out to every scar on her body and face. Yes, I will marry her now." I looked into Mari's eyes and turned back to the bat before new tears could form.

The bat unwrapped himself to his full stature, wings outstretched like an eagle, head held high like a rooster. Only everything was topsy-turvy because the bat was hanging upside down from a perch. Eventually he began to speak.

"Then with the full power invested in me," he said in his most impressive voice, "by the almighty El, by my mighty mother, and by all these motley creatures here below, I now pronounce ye united in mutuality, cohorts in the precious but previously procrastinated progression toward the liberation of the leopard clad lass from her present plight and dire predicament, known very well unto thee both. Only henceforth and thenceforth may ye plight thy troths mutually before me. As translated testament hereto I present thee with this credential to have and to hold from this day forward."

The bat stopped speaking, folded his wings for a moment, then dropped me a note which I stuffed in my pocket and promptly forgot. Mari and I glanced at each other blankly. It seemed as if the bat was going back to sleep so we assumed we were married and kissed each other firmly.

The thought of going back through the spiders or jumping off the roof didn't appeal to either of us so we just ran into the château in the corner of the room. And what better place for a honeymoon than a French château, now I ask you?

The entrance floor was so clean and shiny we could see our reflections – actually just one reflection, we were clinging so closely to one another. I was afraid I'd slip on the glassy surface and bring us both down.

"Welcome to Château Marié," said an image of Marta in the tiles by our feet. "How sweet, you'll be wanting the bridal suite then?"

Mari jumped and I jerked my head up. "Of course," I said, "and right away."

"Wonderful," said the ladybug, "then just show me your marriage certificate. It's only a formality. But you can't be too careful these days, even in France."

Marriage certificate? Oh, she must be meaning that scrap of paper from the bat. Let's see if I still had it stuffed in my pants somewhere. At last I retrieved it and handed it over. She unfolded it ceremoniously, grinning from ear to ear, which, granted, is not much of a distance in a ladybug.

After quite a long and frustrating time reading it, she raised her head, shook it, and said, "I'm sorry, but the bridal suite is not available for you two. But I have two other rooms which might suit your fancy."

"Why not the bridal suite?!" I demanded, just a bit too harshly now that I think about it.

Marta looked embarrassed. "Well, according to the way I read this document, you're not really married," she said.

"What?" I said and grabbed the paper.

Sure enough here's what it said in unmistakable bat scrawl:

Translation of formal proceedings before
His Singular Presence the bat:
Get Mary first, then get married.

I showed it to Mari and she started to cry.

"Hey, it doesn't say I can't marry you. It only says we need to rescue Mary first."

"Well, we'd better get on with it then," said Mari, heading blindly down the hall.

"Don't you want the rooms?" cried Marta to the back of my head.

"Not at present it seems," I said.

"Oh I forgot," she yelled as we were turning the knob of the first door, "you're brother is back from the war. You'll probably find him in the TV room."

~24~
Closer to Mary

Did I tell you that after he left the dollhouse, my brother James grew up again to be another Naval officer. Or maybe it was the same Naval officer all over again. I'm not sure how that worked out in real life. At any rate, he rose again to the rank of Lieutenant Commander and again he lived on an aircraft carrier, flying jet fighters. Oddly enough, though, this time he hated jellyrolls.

Every so often he would come visit me in Aunt Clara's old house. All he wanted was a good fruit pie. Or several of them, I should say. I'd bring some home from the restaurant that had gotten too old to sell. James would eat them anyway. Why he'd even eat them if they'd fallen on the floor. He wondered how I avoided getting fat working in a restaurant. I told him it was because I didn't particularly care for food of my own making.

"Brother," he would say, "here I am Lieutenant Commander James of the U.S. Navy, while you're still Little Nobody William of Frankie's Chicken. The only thing we have in common is that we both wear white uniforms. Why don't you get an exciting life like mine? The thrill, the danger, yes, even the romance of desperate struggles with men and machines, don't you ever long for that?

I'd tell him it's struggle enough to serve hungry customers properly.

"Oh William," he'd say, "what can I say? Maybe we both need to find girls and get married. That'd settle me down and fire you up!"

I seriously doubted he'd ever slow up for a girl, or that a girl'd ever show up for me. So we just continued for many years in our separate lives until, as time would have it, we ended up in the same dollhouse once again.

At least that's what Marta had just told me. My brother was here! I grabbed Mari's hand immediately and we headed down the hall.

"Oh Marta," I yelled over my shoulder, "where's the TV room?"

"Turn right at the statue of Ladybug Johnson," she said, "Right there turn left, then it's at the end of the hall, right by the statue of Ladybug Godiva."

Confusing to you? Well whatever. At any rate we turned right instead of left. At the end of the hall was a room with computer monitors which looked enough like TV's to beckon us in. And there, in one of the monitors, big as life was my very own Mary wearing a leopard skin. The thing was complete with long tail and cute little ears. I was amazed at how well Mary looked as a cat. I couldn't help staring at her until Mari gave me a poke.

"She looks slinky and happy," said Mari, "maybe we should just leave her in there."

I grabbed the mouse and clicked on a dialog box. Suddenly we could hear Mary.

"Who clicked on me?" she said, "Is that you Willy? I can't see anything. There are no monitors in here."

"Yes, we're here to rescue you," piped up Mari. "If you really want, that is."

"Who's that with you?" asked Mary.

"His fiancée," said Mari – a bit too forcefully.

"His *financier?*" Mary cried, "I can't hear. You're breaking up. William, are you out there? What's going on? When are you coming for me?"

"Mary," I said, "how do we get in there to rescue you? Where are you?"

"You have to get into the tiny cottage at the end of the main hall," said Mary. "Stick your hair in first and you'll be all right. Hey, who's that with you?"

"We're on our way then," I said, "no time to lose."

"But who's…" But I'd already flipped off the computer.

"Let's go. Hurry!" I said, pulling Mari's hand once again through the halls. That's when I noticed that she had a noticeable limp.

"Oh, I'm sorry," I said taking her arm. "We'll just walk at your pace, okay?"

She just smiled at me and squeezed my waist.

When we got to the cottage we almost stepped on it, it was so small. We knelt down as if looking for a lost ring on the floor.

"That's too small to get into," said Mari. "Shrinking so small will crush us to death."

"Mary got in," I said.

"That doesn't mean we have to risk our lives," said Mari. "Who is this Mary anyway? An old girlfriend?"

"She's not old," I said, sticking a strand of the hair on my wrist into the tiny open doorway.

Suddenly I disappeared right before Mari's eyes. She jumped back in fright, but then put her eye up to the door to see if she could see me. In doing so, one of her eyelashes entered the doorway and poof, there she was beside me in the cottage.

"Well I guess it works!" she said breathlessly.

We noticed the big bed under the window and Mari flopped down on it instinctively. "There's plenty of room for you on *this* one," she said.

I said I thought not, but she was already preoccupied with something she felt through the covers. She coaxed it up to the pillows and took it in her hand.

"Will," she squealed, "remember how you never gave me a diamond for our engagement?"

"Uh huh," I said, already distracted by the computer keyboard I had just discovered.

"Well I have found one, may I have it?"

"Uh, sure, anything," I said distractedly.

"It needs a setting."

"Yeah, okay," I muttered.

"Open the drawer under the computer."

122

This I did without even realizing that it was not Mari speaking, but the 'diamond' she was holding.

There in the center of the drawer was a single gold solitaire setting. I picked it up, turned around and gave it to Mari who was wearing an astonished expression.

"The ring talked," she said. "I mean the diamond in it." Yes, the diamond had already jumped into the setting and Mari had wasted no time in putting it on her finger.

I looked at the ring and the diamond was indeed beautiful – brilliant, colorless but not without flaw. But its only blemish was in the shape of a smiley face which glowed a bit and smiled a bit too much.

"Hi, my name is Lee Bola." It smiled.

Lee tried to get me to wear a ring made from his wife 'Lea Bola' but I said I wasn't interested.

"Saving your ring finger for Mary?" he asked.

"No, for me," injected Mari immediately. "Now please show me how to find this elusive leopard."

The ring on her hand gave her a pleasurable feeling, like pasting it with BenGay or something. It guided her to the keyboard and then over it like a piano player. Soon she and I were inside the computer and being outfitted with avatars. For me, I chose a lion again, so Mari naturally chose a lioness.

"Its more regal than a leopard, don't you think?" she purred.

Actually I was thinking that fashion-wise, a leopard or a cheetah would be much more daring. But I just nodded my head in agreement. I had to admit we made a handsome couple, the lion and his lioness.

~25~
Cat Fight

With the ring on her finger, or paw actually, Mari knew exactly where to guide us. She had no trouble locating the closet of costumes, and we bounded through to the back where the animal skins were kept. There indeed was Mary, dancing about with a black panther. Of course it was only the skin of a panther whereas here was I showing up with a real live, flesh and blood lioness. Or at least the avatar of a lioness. Or I should say the lioness was an avatar of a girl. I guess that only made it worse, showing up with a girl. Actually I hadn't thought of it until now. Oh well, here they were face to face and not even waiting for me to introduce them properly.

"Who are *you*?" said Mary to the lioness, without even glancing at me.

"We're here to rescue you," said Mari.

"We? Who's *we*?" demanded Mary.

"*We*, my lion and me," said Mari, nudging me a bit.

I just stood there stupidly. I had absolutely no experience handling big cats, especially when they are fighting. I figured the best thing for me to do was to try and stay out of it.

"He happens to be my lion, I tamed him," said Mary, staring over into my eyes.

"You're not even a lion," said Mari, "you're covered with silly spots. Do you have chicken pox?"

"Oh this old thing," she said throwing off the leopard skin. "Actually I'm really a girl, unlike you apparently."

The lioness was taken aback because Mary was indeed a real girl. In fact she was just as striking as Mari had been under the influence of her wand.

"Step back, fuzzy-face," said Mary, "I'm riding my lion outta here."

"You'll ride nothing," said Mari, "you'll walk behind my tail and when we're free of this place you can attend our wedding."

"Is this true?" asked Mary, glaring again at me. "She's nothing but a lying lion."

"First I'm taking you both out of here," I said, "then we'll all sort things out."

"I think we should settle things right here and now," said Mari. "A lioness can tear a girl to shreds. And often does."

The lioness then backed Mary into a corner and bared her teeth. Her breath poured over the girl's face like heat from an oven. But Mary held her gaze.

"You'll never get a man with breath like that," said Mary. "What have you been eating? And let me see your paws."

"What about my paws?" said Mari.

"Well your nails are a sickening yellow. Where have you been walking? Would you be interested in a few beauty tips?"

"I don't need them, I already have my man," said Mari.

"But for how long?" said Mary, "how long do you think he'll put up with your smelly lion's breath? I know a mouthwash that even works on dogs and cats."

"Really?" said Mari, "where can I get it?"

"Well," said Mary, "it's called 'Litterine' but you can't get it on the internet. I'd be glad to show you where you *can* get it. When we get out of here, that is."

"Oh would you?" said Mari, 'thanks. And something for my nails as well?"

"Sure!" said Mary, "come on let's just get out of this place! You know, we could go faster if you'd let me ride on your back."

"Sure!" said Mari, "will you take me to a real shopping mall? They don't have them in the country I come from."

"Of course," said Mary, although she'd never been to one either.

So the two bounded off, in eager anticipation of a big lady's day in the shops. I don't think either of them gave me a second thought as they careened through the various chat rooms and cyber halls on their way out. I straggled along behind, struggling to understand women.

My brain began to spin at this impossible task. How *do* I get myself into such predicaments? To me, the thought of shopping in a mall with two fighting cats was far from appealing. It was appalling.

Finally we reached the portal where we first came in. We were about to log off when Lee Bola spoke up from the ring on Mari's paw.

"Wait," he said, "don't log off before I bake a cookie for you."

"Why do we need a cookie?" demanded Mary.

"Without a cookie I won't know your names when you come back," he replied. "You see, your names and all sorts of other information about you is baked into your cookie. I keep the cookies right here in my special computer cookie jar."

None of us liked the idea of Lee Bola, or Vick Cyrus or any of their sparkly friends for that matter, having information on us. So we put Mari's ring back into the drawer in the computer table. It protested incessantly but shut up when we closed the drawer on it. Then we just logged off.

It was then that Mari and I turned back into a girl and a boy. Mary, who's avatar was already a girl, just turned back into herself. The two girls then merrily jumped out of the cottage and headed down the hall, hand in hand. All the while they talked nonstop about nail polish, mascara and pimple cream.

"Oh Mari," said Mary, "I don't mean to walk so fast. I didn't realize you have a limp. Where did you get it?"

"I was tortured because the rat king didn't want me for his bride."

"Oh how sad," said Mary, "why don't you take Willy here. He's no king, not even a prince, but at least he's not a rat."

"Oh, but I wouldn't want to take him away from you," said Mari, "you've been long lost sweethearts for all these years."

"Well then it's your turn!" said Mary. "You have him. I can find someone more interesting, I'm sure."

I felt about two feet tall, hearing all this. Actually we were even much smaller than that.

~26~
The Prisoner[1]

James sat dejectedly in the TV room. There were six TVs in the room each with its own cluster of comfortable chairs. All the TVs were on, but when you changed the channel on one, they all changed. Of course that didn't matter to James. All the channels were the same to him. He shut them off and all the screens went blank. He was alone in the room. He was alone with his thoughts. He was afraid of being alone so he picked up a magazine. He noticed that there was an article on the war in it. So he leafed lazily to it, started reading but then succumbed to his own thoughts about the war. They made for much more spellbinding entertainment.

"I was flying my 38th mission over the gook capital," he reminisced, "when a surface-to-air missile took off my right wing. I ejected and landed right in a pond in the center of the city. Lots of people gathered around and fished me out. The crowd started kicking me. My leg was broken but they paraded me through the streets anyway. They carried my helmet on a stick and my uniform like a scarecrow. I was in my underpants.

"I was taken to the main prison and placed in a tiny room all by myself. For a bed there was a straw mat on the floor. No pillow, no blanket. For toilet facilities there was a rusty metal bucket with a lid that didn't fit. No toilet paper of course. They came and emptied the bucket every few days. For food there was pumpkin soup, or on special occasions, bean soup. Now you must understand that bean soup is just beans boiled in water. No meat whatsoever. Still, it was a welcome change from the pumpkin. I lost a lot of weight.

"Then for five years I was tortured to reveal military information. They would scar my face with a razor blade. But I told them only my name, rank, serial number and date of birth. Then they got mad and ripped out my fingernails.

"'Why do you disrespect the guards so much?' they asked me. I told them that it was because the guards treated me like an animal. So they punched me a few times, broke my nose, and put a metal collar around my neck. From time to time I was made to sleep in a small bamboo cage suspended from the ceiling.

"Then came the 'peace visitors' from all over the world. They wanted to make peace and forget about the reasons we went to war in the first place. Actually I don't remember those reasons very well right now. But they must have been good ones. My captors tortured me so that I wouldn't tell the visitors that I was being tortured. When I told the visitors the truth, my captors ripped out my toenails. For five years they mistreated me this way, trying to make me thank them publically for treating me well. I would never do that because it would be telling a lie.

"The only thing that ever helped was talking to God. I didn't ask Him for super-human strength, or that He would strike the enemies dead. No, I asked Him only for courage, comfort and control through it all. He did help me quite a bit. After the war I meant to thank Him but never really got around to it.

"Finally the enemy agreed to send me home. When I arrived home I was again paraded through the streets. This time I got to wear my bright new dress uniform, but nevertheless, I walked with a noticeable limp and could wave at the crowds with only my left arm. My face was scarred and my nose had been reconstructed. They didn't do such a great job.

"After all this fanfare I was discharged from the Navy with lots of well wishes and two weeks severance pay. I had nowhere to go. Where would I get a job? Who would hire a one-armed jet pilot?

"So I headed off to my brothers house. Everyone on the bus stared at my nose. I was too tired to care. My brother wasn't home so I broke the latch on the back door and had a seat in his small den. I tried to turn on the old radio but could only get static. The knob came off in my hand so I had to unplug the radio from the wall. All I wanted was a nice piece of pie. Eventually I fell asleep on the loveseat. I was there for two days with my legs curled up.

"I finally awoke and my brother still wasn't home. I thought of going upstairs and trying on some costumes, like I had done when I was a little boy. I think it was

God who let me into the dollhouse because He likes to comfort the weary and the broken. I was both of those. I just wanted to be somebody else – anybody else.

"The Ladybug Marta saw immediately what bad shape I was in.

"'Oh James,' she said, 'I see the war has been most unkind to you. Did you forget to take along your trusty sword?'

"'I was after glory,' I admitted, 'but what I got instead was gory. I hate swords now.'

"'So are you ready to take a wife at last?' she asked. 'If so, you've come to the right place. I happen to have several rooms with lovely, lonely girls in them.'

"'Do you have any pigs who would love my nose?' I asked.

"I looked so dejected the ladybug sent me directly up to the bat, even though it was mid-day and he'd probably be asleep. On the way up even the ugly spiders shied away from me.

"Upstairs the bat took one look and accidently fell from his perch.

"'Just as well,' he said, 'come close. I don't want to have to shout this. When animals come into misfortune we say that it is El who is punishing them for doing something bad. But I'm not sure that's always true. El's ways are mysterious. Are you being punished by God? Have you done something bad?'

"'No! Or well – yes', I said, 'I lived for glory, not for God."

"'I see. So what do you live for now?' asked the bat.

"'Nothing,' I replied.

"'So why are you here?' asked the bat.

"'I just want to put on one of your masks and hide behind a colorful costume,' I said. 'Maybe that will attract a girl for me, and make me feel better.'

"'No mask will heal the hurt inside you,' said the bat, 'and no woman would have the outside. You are in a real mess. So what about God?"

"'God helped me out a bit,' I said, 'but He also let all of this happen in the first place, so I guess you could say I'm mad at Him."

"'Then I have a perfect place for you to rest and find yourself again,' said the bat, 'and maybe find God again too. It's called the TV room."

"'That doesn't sound like a very restful place,' I said.

"'In this mansion,' said the bat, 'nobody ever goes into the TV room. Everything is reruns or commercials. Even the commercials are reruns. So you'll be quite undisturbed, I assure you.'

"I thanked the bat and followed the ant guide he provided. Soon we arrived in the TV room. The journey was without incident. The spiders were still avoiding me and I even heard cockroaches sniggering. There was not a mouse to be seen anywhere.

"I sat down dejectedly and turned on a TV. I soon tired of that so I looked at a magazine. I soon tired of that so I picked up a book. It was this book in fact. Before coming into this crazy house I didn't realize it was possible read a book and be in it at the same time. But I guess even that's possible because there I was doing it. Yet I soon tired of even that so I placed lots of chair cushions on the floor and fell fast asleep.

~27~
The Reunion

Mary and Mari were heading out the front door of the château when I piped up from behind, "Hey girls, remember my brother? He's in here. In the TV room."

"Yes, how exciting," said Mari, "a brother. Is he as handsome as you?"

"He's a pirate," interjected Mary.

"Oh that's even more exciting,' said Mari. "Let's go see this pirate! Does he have a black eye patch?"

Mary wasn't all that thrilled at the prospect of seeing James again but she dawdled along after us anyway. After getting some faulty directions from a centipede we nevertheless came upon the TV room. Entirely by accident. There was James, fast asleep on some chair cushions he had placed on the floor.

I was shocked to see his scarred face. I was horrified to see his deformed nose. It made him snore. I was going to wake him up but Mary stopped me. She bent down and placed a gentle hand on his shoulder but didn't stir him. A tear fell on his shirt, then another. After a while she rose.

"I'll meet you by the front door," she said, and left the room hurriedly.

Mari gave me a curious glance but then knelt down by the sleeping James herself. Without touching him, she placed her hand over his messy hair and over his scarred face. Her eyes became moist.

"Like me," she said, "you are a fallen warrior. Like me, you sacrificed yourself in service to your country. Like me, you fell into foul hands. Like me, you are now scarred in body, soul and spirit.

"How can we hope to live in this modern world?" she continued. "It only belongs to the beautiful. How can we cope with others who remain unscathed, but shy away from the battle? How can we respect these glittery people who hide instead of fight?"

Then she bent down and tenderly kissed him awake.

"Get up, my dear warrior," she said, lifting his arm into her lap, "arise into my company, and bask in the love of someone who feels for your every injury and scar. Inside and out, I am with you. Past and present, I am there. Real and imagined, I am by your side. And share in my wounds as well, as my officer, my commander, my constant companion."

James looked sleepily into her eyes and knew, at last he had found a home. "My princess at last," he said. "Like in a fairy tale." They didn't have to say anything more to each other. Their eyes said it all.

Just then Marta entered the room, breaking up the embrace. "How touching," she said, "but don't think you're married yet. Get your derrières outside at once and present yourselves to the bat. There's no time to waste when you're in this state. But first pick up those cushions and put them back on the chairs."

I just sat there stunned. It was all happening too fast. I was going to get left behind once again by the rush of events. Like when Katherine got married. You'd think my sister would give me some advance warning. But no. She just told me to rent some nice clothes and show up on Saturday. Then off they disappeared and there I was alone again. Another wedding all giggles and smiles, and none of them mine.

Standing by the front door, Mary felt the same way when James and Mari rushed shamelessly past her and out into the bat's chambers. They were giggling and smiling so much the bat had to clear his throat to get their attention.

"Hrmmm," he said, "it's obvious you two are here to get married. Hrmmm, what wedding ceremony number would be best for you two? Let's see. Hrmmm. Well actually there's none, so I'll just wing it. Ha-ha. Get it? Hrmmm."

But Mari and James were too enwrapped in each other to pay any attention whatsoever.

"Whatever," said the bat. "Well here goes: Dearly beloved roaches, spiders, ants and other invited and uninvited guests, greetings. These two people may look old for their ages, but they have had hard lives. Many people in difficult and painful circumstances may turn to the Bible in search of comfort and guidance. El has graciously given these His children an assurance that He will provide sustained support through every season of life. 'The faithful love of the Lord never ends! His mercies never cease. Great is His faithfulness; His mercies begin afresh each morning.' (Lamentations 3:22-23).

"El truly is faithful. In other words, all can count on Him to be and do all He says. For example, the Bible assures us that El is trustworthy, loving, and never makes mistakes (Psalm 37:5; Romans 5:8; Joshua 1:5). He will guide these two safely through all life's dangers. Hardships such as theirs may indeed cause some believers to question El's dependability, but we can trust Him because He knows all things. He's aware of the length and strength of their current affliction and the purpose in it. He also uses His knowledge to offer them the best possible help and support. What's more, El is all-powerful to meet needs and change situations according to His plan. And He is everywhere, including right beside them in whatever they face, whatever they must bear. He says, 'I will never fail you. I will never abandon you.'" (Hebrews 13:5).

Then the bat looked directly at them and unfurled his wings partway. "Therefore I charge you two to place your trust in the all-seeing, all-powerful, ever-present El. As humans possessing spirits, you can know this El more fully as God, and even Father. We animals in this book are only partially, and dimly aware of Him as El. I must confess that the real animals outside this book are not even conscious of Him at all. And many *people* outside this book don't believe in Him either. But God is real. Put your trust in Him and His Son's payment for your rejection of Him. Only then can you awaken tomorrow with a fresh sense of His faithfulness to carry you through the rest of your lives together. Only you can worship Him in this way. And only He can change you from the inside out."

Here the bat fell silent and the couple wondered if the ceremony was over. "Are we married yet?" asked James.

"James and Mari," began the bat again, "do you take each other to be your lawful wedded halves, to have and to hold on to, to be whole until one of you departs this life?"

"We do," they said.

"Even when you get sick and tired of each other?" asked the bat.

"Even then," they answered. "With God's help."

"Then with all the power vested and invested in me," the bat said in his most impressive voice, and stretching his wings out even more, "by the almighty El, by my mighty mother superior, and by all these motley creatures here below, I now pronounce ye united in mutuality, cohorts in the precious state of matrimonial bonds, solid and unbreakable by man or beast." Here the bat fell silent again, almost as if he were out of breath.

"Are we married yet?" asked James.

"Aye, aye sir," said the bat, "you're married. And here's the paper to prove it. But don't kiss her just yet. It offends the spiders and I'm not too thrilled with the custom myself."

~28~
The Conservatory

Mary and I expected James and his new bride to immediately dash out of the dollhouses and into the wonderful wide world waiting outside. True, they were disfigured, scarred, but they had each other. Yet instead of the freedom afforded by the real world, they headed back into the safety of the château with its artificial masks and fantasy costumes.

"Welcome to Château Éludé," said Marta at the doorway, "you have made a wise decision to elude the outside world. Did you know that it's actually cursed? That's what the bat said anyway. But you can rest easy in here. Our masks cover a multitude of syndromes and our costumes a whole plethora of personality disorders. They also make you look nice. And when you look nice you feel nice, and when you feel nice, you *are* nice. And that makes the task of marriage much more manageable, even enjoyable at times. If you can believe that."

The new couple shrugged their shoulders and headed gleefully down the hall to the costume room. This left

Marta alone with Mary. "Well Mary," said Marta, "are you glad it's not you that's married!"

"Not really," said Mary, "but I'd have to have the right Prince Appealing."

"Oh they're all appealing at first," said Marta, "at least mine were. But man-ladybugs just don't seem very manly after a week or so. They go off color. They change their spots. They turn into stink bugs and their devotion to you becomes spotty at best. You know, I'd rather have a stag beetle anytime. They're so shiny black and dangerous looking. Big too."

"Have you ever had a stag beetle?" asked Mary, wrinkling her nose.

"Well no," admitted Marta, "but just thinking about it makes my spots dance."

Just then I emerged from the hall leading to the TV room. "Oh William," said Marta, "I was just going to set Mary here up with a stag beetle husband. Do you think she could handle one?"

"She can marry whomever she chooses," I said coolly.

Mary gave me a cold look. "I think we need to talk," she said. "Would you care to come with me to the conservatory?"

"What's a conservatory?" I enquired.

"It's a greenhouse for growing and displaying plants," she replied. "Of course there's no real sunlight in this house so all the plants are artificial. Plastic. Or rubber I believe. But there *is* a nice bench in there to sit and talk on. And plastic plants can't overhear secret conversations."

"Do you have a secret to tell me?" I asked.

"Well maybe, we'll see."

"Then we'd better be off to the conservatory," I said, "before Marta's spots begin to spin."

The conservatory was quite beautiful. Its tall walls and domed ceiling were made entirely of glass panes held together by thin metal frames. Light slanted in from many angles giving the outside a kaleidoscopic appearance. The flowers inside were silk, not plastic and tastefully arranged in rows. You could almost smell them. But not quite, of course. A rose, red and rich-looking was given to Mary by a butterfly as we entered.

142

A beautiful boardwalk meandered throughout the garden and there were benches every so often, love seats actually, where couples could sit and talk. They had ornate iron legs and smooth wooden slats on the seats. Each had a lovely, soft, embroidered cushion which looked almost too nice to place your bottom on.

"Welcome to the great outdoors!" said a cowboy. He was grinin' like a possum eatin' a yellow jacket. He came complete with chaps, spurs and two shiny six-guns on his hips. A hand-rolled cigarette hung from his lips. "I ain't really a cowboy," he said, "but nothing in here is really real. Besides there's no cows around to cowboy around. So I just sit here 'n smoke. It's part of my outfit."

"Well I suppose the clothes do make the man," I said. "The cigarette's a nice touch. So what *are* you?"

"I'm in actuality a horsefly," he said. "but without the actual horse."

"Do you have a name, Mister Horsefly?" asked Mary.

"Darn tootin' I do," he said, "in books I'm reckoned as Tabanidae Tabaninae Tabanus, but my best kemosabe just calls me Tabs. I have many dude-friends. Especially since I started usin' silver bullets. It seems that flies attract flies."

"Well Tabs," said Mary, "could you show us to a nice private bench and then fly away like a nice fly?"

"Shucks yes," said Tabs, glancing at me, "it's part of my cowboy code. Never bother another trail-hand's woman."

As we were walking to the secluded bench the horsefly cowboy recited his code to us. We didn't really want to hear it, but out it came nevertheless:

The Code of the Old West

1. Don't talk much; save your breath for breathing.

2. Always tend to your horse's needs before your own.

3. Never pass anyone on the trail without saying "Howdy."

4. Don't stir up dust around the chuck wagon.

5. Remove your guns before sitting at the dining table.

6. Complain about the cooking and you become the cook.

7. Never try on another man's hat, his horse or his woman.

8. Don't inquire into a person's past.

9. Respect the land and the environment by not smoking in hazardous fire areas, disfiguring rocks, trees, or other natural areas. Stay on established trails and camp only in designated campsites. Do not feed the bears.

10. Never shoot a woman or swear in front of her.

I thanked the horsefly cowboy politely and then told him to buzz off. Respectfully of course. I was dying to know the secret Mary wanted to tell me.

But instead of telling me a secret she just stared into my eyes. At first I stared right back but when she didn't say anything I started to squirm. She cocked her head as if expecting me to say something. I had no idea what she wanted me to say.

"Well?" she finally said.

"Well what?" I said right back.

"Well, why did you rescue me?"

I couldn't think of anything to say.

"Twice," she said.

"Because you were trapped?" I offered.

"Like you would rescue a raccoon in a trap?" she asked.

"Yeah, sure." I said, "like that."

She looked down at the path in front of us. "That's what I thought," she muttered.

"What did you say?" I muttered back.

She looked back up into my face and her beautiful green eyes burned into mine. "Do I look like a raccoon to you?"

Suddenly I knew what she was driving at. Suddenly I knew that she was indeed the most lovely girl in the world. Suddenly I knew that I couldn't live without her. Not one minute longer. Suddenly I couldn't breathe. Did I love her? Did I really love her?

"You bet!" I blurted, "I mean *no*. I mean... No, you're even better than a raccoon." Desperately I placed my hand on hers.

Her eyes looked annoyingly at our hands, then shyly she bowed her head and a hint of a smile crossed her lips. "Maybe like a mink?" she said, turning her hand under mine and enfolding our fingers together.

"Oh, much more than a mink," I gasped.

"You're blushing," she said.

"I am *not*," I protested in my most manly voice. But it was probably true. I know it was true about her. She was as colorful as the flowers behind her. I wanted to kiss her but as a twelve-year-old I didn't know how. Okay I knew *how*, but I didn't know, well – the effects it might have or what it might lead to. Also, at twelve it was a fleeting feeling and suddenly I wasn't so sure about the idea of kissing anything. I suppose if we had been sixteen there would have been no hesitation. So we just held hands and silently enjoyed the flowers for a while.

~29~
Finding God

Mary and I were still sitting on the conservatory bench, thinking and holding hands. I was afraid to move my fingers for fear she'd let go. Eventually I must have appeared stiff for she did let go and peered at me inquisitively.

"What's the difference between El and God," she asked out of the blue.

"El is just the Hebrew name for God meaning 'mighty one.'" I said.

"No," she replied, "No, I mean the animals in this house keep referring to an El who made them, but they don't seem to know anything about God."

"I think El and God are one and the same," I said. "In here, El represents the very limited understanding that animals have of God."

"Do you understand God?" she asked.

"Of course, a little bit. He's living inside me. Do you?"

"I think I only know him as El," said Mary, wrinkling her brow.

"Do you know you can know Him personally?" I asked.

"I don't need to," she said, "if he tells you anything, you can tell me."

"It doesn't work that way," I said. "If you don't know Him personally you will go to hell."

"Hey buster," she said, her green eyes gleaming, "I've done many more good things than bad. More good things than you, for instance. If I can't get into heaven then neither can you."

"Being good or doing good things has nothing to do with it," I said. "It's all about whether you've asked Jesus into your heart."

"There are many ways into heaven, Mister Know-It All," she said.

"Who told you that? There's only one way to heaven." I said.

"Okay, you're right," she said, "I figured it out myself. One way. The mice must have one way, the insects one way, and humans one way. Everyone has one way – or another."

"Do different humans have different ways?" I asked.

"No, silly," she said. "All humans would have the same one way."

"Then we agree," I said, "only insects and animals don't go to heaven, as far as I know."

"Sure," she replied, "I can agree with that. There must be an insect heaven and an animal heaven. And all humans must go to the same heaven."

"You're right about human heaven," I said, "but it's not for you."

She looked hurt, and then mad.

"Why not?"

"Because you have rejected God in you heart and you won't let Jesus fix it."

"Yes I will," She said evenly. A full minute passed.

I was silent and presently I saw a tear appear at the corner of her eye. Then another. Soon she was sobbing on my shoulder and telling me how much she had hurt God. It all came out so quickly, like water bursting from a dam.

"But there's good news for you," I said finally.

"What?" she whined, "that you're going to make everything all better."

"No, but *He* is."

"El?" she asked.

"Yes, God," I said, "ask Him to come live inside you."

"He'd do that?"

"In a twinkling of an eye," I said.

Her eyes twinkled. "Should I ask now?"

"Sure," I said, "if you're ready."

So Mary uttered the most important words of her life: "Dear El, I mean God. I know I've disappointed You and have done bad things, said bad things, and thought bad things. I've even pretended You don't exist, when I know very well that You do. Willy here says that You will forgive me if I ask, and come and live inside me. Would You really do that? I mean would You please do that. Pleasey please. I mean *if* You please."

She stopped and bowed her head as if the ceiling might suddenly come crashing down on us. "Willy, did I ask okay?" she asked.

"You prayed wonderfully," I said. "He has done it."

"I know," she said, "He has come into my heart and I am His and only His forever."

We just sat there for the longest time thinking about what had just happened. One tiny question put to God had resulted in a life changed for all time, a soul safe and secure for eternity. If you're reading this book and have already asked that question, then you know what I mean. If you haven't asked the question yet, then what are you waiting for? Go ahead and do it if you're ready. If you please. Don't worry, I'll wait for you right here.

~30~
Knowing God

Mary and I were so excited about her accepting Jesus into her heart that we forgot all about ourselves and just talked about Him. She had a thousand questions for me. No maybe closer to a million. I ended up telling her the whole story: how God created the angels to love and be with Him. How the head angel decided to take over God's position. How he and all his followers were thrown out of heaven. Then how God created men and women to also love Him and be with Him. But they too rebelled and thought they'd do things their way. So God had to separate Himself from them too, which is called death. This was their punishment. To be without God is to be in constant torture. This separation was torture for God too. It made Him so sad that He made an entire nation of people out of the descendants of just one man. He called this nation His 'chosen people' Israel, and gave them all the laws necessary to live their lives pleasing to Him. He wanted to love them so much. All He asked for was their love and obedience in return. But they failed miserably (we all do) so He sent His only Son, Jesus to take on their death sentence. This Jesus did willingly on the cross. He took on the punishment due to every man, woman and child on the earth. And believe me the crucifixion was torture of the most awful kind imaginable. More pain and suffering than we could ever dream up. Not just being nailed to a cross and dying naked in the baking sun – but even worse, being torn apart from His Father God, with whom He is one. That meant that God died that day.

Mary and I cried as we thought of it. Jesus did this for us. He stood in our place and got what we deserved. We should have died. We should have been nailed to the cross. But now instead we're going to be in heaven with God forever. We'll be ruling with Jesus. We'll be with Him getting what He deserves, a place at the right hand of the Father. Why? Well, since Jesus never did anything bad against His Father, and since He was still God, He had the power to break the hold of death on Him. He rose from the dead and is now back united with the Father again in heaven. He's waiting for us to join Him there. When we die we don't become ghosts or angels or anything like that. The Bible says that our spirits go immediately up to be with Jesus. Isn't that wonderful? Then someday soon Jesus will be coming back to earth to reign as king. And we'll all reign with Him.

"But what about those who don't ask Jesus into their hearts?" asked Mary.

"They only get what they deserve," I said.

"Hell?"

"That's right."

"Even if they're good people?" she asked.

"No human being today can measure up to God's standards," I said. "That's what the Bible says. We have to rely on how good and perfect Jesus is. He brings us to God like a groom brings in his bride. White and spotless. Blameless. Beautiful."

"Which means everyone should ask Him into their heart, right?" said Mary.

"Yes, I'm so glad we've both done that, my love," I said.

Oops. The 'L' word had slipped out accidently but there it was, out in the open for her to deal with. I was suddenly afraid. What would she say? What *could* she say? I looked away red-faced.

"Why Willy," she said, "you're red as a beet. Are you having a heart attack?"

"I suppose you might call it that," I said. Or an attack of the heart. I felt totally defeated. No dignity left whatsoever. Completely vanquished and trembling under her thumb. I'd lost the upper hand. At such a young age, this boy-girl stuff was just a game for us. Would she go in for the kill or show me mercy?

As it turned out she did neither.

~31~
The Bat's Last Word

I had just called Mary "my love" and now I was waiting for her response. Would she laugh? Would she get angry, or worse yet, would she just ignore it? Well, like I said, she did none of these things. She took my hand again and said:

"I too am glad we both know Jesus, because if we didn't I don't think I should be sitting here this close to you. And I don't think I should be holding your hand like this. And I don't think I should be telling you that I kinda like you either."

"Really, are you telling me that?" I stammered.

"Do you speak English?"

"Yes."

"Then what part of 'I kinda like you' don't you understand?

"I don't understand how you could choose me," I said.

"I didn't choose you," she said, "El, I mean God did. And He is bringing me to you to be a friend. Maybe as a reward for rescuing me. How should I know? But here I am."

"Maybe it's because I kinda like you too," I said.

"Maybe so." She agreed.

We were just about to kiss, and I know this is supposed to be the best part of the book, but I'm sorry. Our ages got in the way again. You know, the yuck factor "kiss a girl" thing. And the yuck factor "put your lips *anywhere* on a boy" thing.

"Willy," she said, "you weren't trying to get fresh, were you?"

"What, with you" I said, "get real."

"Willy," she said, "I hate being twelve. My emotions go haywire. I give up. Do you want to be sixteen and see what happens?"

"Sure I'd like to be sixteen with you," I said, "but that's still to young to marry."

"Oh I see," she said blushing. "I understand. Would eighteen do?"

"Splendidly," I said and we hurried off to see Marta. Then we'd pay a visit to the bat.

Mary knew right where to find Ivanhoho and of course all her creature friends were already gathered for the big ceremony. News in the dollhouses is passed primarily by chemicals which travel lightningly fast down lines of ants which weave everywhere. Everyone knew not only of the impending wedding, but also every detail of the courtship which preceded it. Most could not understand how anyone could marry a person without having kissed them first. What if they bit, or sucked, or tasted bad? But oh well, humans were strange creatures, especially those with God living in them.

As the new couple approached, the bat motioned them to take a seat in a corner of the room over by the spiders. The corner by the spiders was always the least occupied.

"As we were saying," said the bat, "until the couple arrives we shall go over the Ten Tenets For Humans From The Harmony Code.

"But they're already here," piped up Luucy, "wouldn't it be more polite to let them speak first?"

"Yes pleasey," said Shcandelaria."

"Well then, of course," said the bat. Turning to me he said, "I see you have a human Bible with you. It would be so instructive for us if you could read from it your 10 Commandments of God."

I said I'd be glad to but asked if Mary could read, since she had a much more pleasing voice. This idea was met with universal approval and even applause, although insects and mice can't make much noise doing so. This is because all of their hands are really feet. So Mary began reading from Exodus 20:

The Ten Commandments

1 Then God gave the people all these instructions:
[1] 2 "I am the LORD your God, who rescued you from the land of Egypt, the place of your slavery.
3 "You must not have any other god but Me.
[2] 4 "You must not make for yourself an idol of any kind or an image of anything in the heavens or on

156

the earth or in the sea. 5 You must not bow down to them or worship them, for I, the LORD your God, am a jealous God who will not tolerate your affection for any other gods. I lay the sins of the parents upon their children; the entire family is affected—even children in the third and fourth generations of those who reject Me. 6 But I lavish unfailing love for a thousand generations on those who love Me and obey My commands.

[3] 7 "You must not misuse the name of the LORD your God. The LORD will not let you go unpunished if you misuse His name.

[4] 8 "Remember to observe the Sabbath day by keeping it holy. 9 You have six days each week for your ordinary work, 10 but the seventh day is a Sabbath day of rest dedicated to the LORD your God. On that day no one in your household may do any work. This includes you, your sons and daughters, your male and female servants, your livestock, and any foreigners living among you. 11 For in six days the LORD made the heavens, the earth, the sea, and everything in them; but on the seventh day He rested. That is why the LORD blessed the Sabbath day and set it apart as holy.

[5] 12 "Honor your father and mother. Then you will live a long, full life in the land the LORD your God is giving you.

[6] 13 "You must not murder.

[7] 14 "You must not commit adultery.

[8] 15 "You must not steal.

[9] 16 "You must not testify falsely against your neighbor.

[10] 17 "You must not covet your neighbor's house. You must not covet your neighbor's wife, male or female servant, ox or donkey, or anything else that belongs to your neighbor."

The bat thanked Mary and then had Adeylia read from the Harmony Code. Adeylia of all people! The little miss perfect mouse princess. But Mary, standing beside her man, didn't even care that Adeylia stepped right in front of her to read her piece, or that she made a point of reading a little louder, a little slower, and with a little more expression.

Ten Tenets For Humans From The Harmony Code:

1. El is supreme but He lets you make the decisions sometimes.
2. El is timeless but He is always here and never late.
3. El is everywhere but you can keep Him out of your heart.
4. El is invisible but you can see when He is with you.
5. El never changes but if you ask He may change His mind.
6. El is good but He will give you a whack when you need it.
7. El knows everything but He can forget about your mistakes.
8. El created space and time and delicately placed all His creations there.

9. El would die for His most treasured creature, you. And He did. Because you abandoned Him. But He arose to life. So can you.

10. El is one body with all His people and they are one body with each other.

After Adeylia had finished reading, the bat cleared his throat and said, "Assembled creatures, caricatures, avatars and emoticons, we have once again heard the Harmony Code from El Himself. We know it is too deep to understand or even to study. But we are content to hear it anyway, aren't we? And this way we never get into arguments over it, do we? So praise be to El who in His wisdom and discretion has made us content with our ignorance and apathy, even carefree in our instinctive complacency…" Here the bat fell asleep and everyone waited politely until his nap was over. There are certain benefits to being old, partially hairless and presumably in charge of the household.

When he finally stirred Marta piped up, "You'd better marry these two human lovebirds quick before they lock lips out of wedlock. I let them be eighteen and it's all the rage at that age."

Luucy was enraged, "Are there no standards anymore; are there no principles? Are morals passé? Are we to act like animals?"

"But we *are* animals!" said Adeylia.

"I'll speak to you later young lady," said Luucy.

"Now, now," said the bat, "the point is moot. They're here to get married and married they shall be. And rightly so. Just look at them. See what that Château

Masquerade has done to them. They're perfect. Attractive, witty, sensitive, attractive, compassionate, playful, attractive. Why they're action figure collectables. See, they've collected each other. And what's more, in here they can stay this way forever. They will never wear out."

"Uh, actually," I interjected, "I was just thinking we might want to leave this dollhouse and make our way in the real world outside."

This idea was met with universal distain and even hissing, although most insects can't hiss because their mouthparts are so far apart and they lack lips.

"If you leave this house, William," said the bat, "you must know that you will revert to your real age, which is fifty." Everyone gasped. Mary immediately wondered if she'd become the old wart lady again. She looked at the bat fearfully and with pleading eyes.

"You must tell him everything," said the bat.

"Willy," said Mary slowly, "I was not always as young and beautiful as I am now."

"Oh, that doesn't matter…" I started to say. But she pressed on.

"No Willy, let me speak. I was *really* ugly, inside and out. I had warts on my nose."

Once again I started to protest but she cut me off.

"No Willy, wait. There's more. I'm your Aunt Clara's sister."

I was stunned. "But my Aunt Clara's sister was my…"

"Yes Willy," said Mary in a thin voice, "my recollection is hazy but I was kept in a small room on

160

the third floor of Aunt Clara's house until I made friends with a mouse and entered this enchanted mansion. That's when I became young and you rescued me. Yes Willy, I'm your Aunt Clara's sister and therefore I must be your – grandmother. I didn't think it would matter in here, but if we go outside it will be, well really really awkward.

I was shocked. I was not too thrilled about marrying my grandmother, even in an enchanted mansion. You see there's this thing about not marrying your own flesh and blood. It's strictly taboo and verboten. That means don't do it. Don't even kiss them. I mean romantically, not the way I kiss my sister Katherine. I stared at Mary as if I didn't even know her and she began to weep softly.

Just at that time a tiny bug dragged himself out the front door of the château and absentmindedly took a seat next to Shcandelaria.

"Am I late? I've come a long way," he whispered to her before realizing that she was an ugly spider. But then it was too late to move. Still, being a booklouse, he wasn't all that attractive himself, even in his academic robe and funny hat. So Shcandelaria in her sweet way told him everything that had happened so far.

"But oh, wait!" he exclaimed, jumping up and knocking the spider head over eight heels. "Stop proceeding with the proceedings!"

"Why in El's name?" yelled the bat.

"Let the louse speak," said Luucy, "it's only polite."

"Okay," said the bat, "then speak, you louse."

The professor gathered his courage. "Gathered friends and fellows, as you know I'm a booklouse," said the booklouse, "and as such I devour tons of books and papers. Even legal papers. Now I just happen to remember a certain adoption certificate certifying that our Mary here was in fact adopted by William's great grandparents. Other papers state categorically that she became one of *three* sisters, namely Aunt Clara, William's grandmother, and herself. Her Last Will and Testament, which I unfortunately ate only yesterday attested to the fact that she had no husbands and no children. So therefore and consequently and by reason of deduction I can ascertain, deduce and pronounce that Mary is of no blood relation to William whatsoever. However this evidence does shed light on how he could rescue her as a kinsman redeemer.

Everyone seemed relieved and overjoyed by this news, especially Mary and myself. Again we almost kissed but in the nick of time spied Luucy staring at us. So we just kissed in our imaginations.

"Well kids," chimed in the bat, "while we're spreading good news about like guano, I have something to add. William, if you marry Mary in here and then leave the house, she would only become your age, no older. The harmony code ascribes some of the husband's attributes to the wife by association. This is how some humans can become blameless through union with Christ.

Mary and I gazed at each other. Here we were eighteen, hot and in love. Why should we give all this up? Weren't we already living everyone's dream? Well for one thing, isn't reality better than a mere dream? And also, dreams lack several important things: Significance. Meaning and purpose in life. The chance to leave a legacy behind after you die. The privilege of serving God and other people. None of this can happen in a dream. Dreams are very self-centered things. I could tell Mary was thinking about these things too.

"I'd rather be old and real," she said, "than young and fake. If I can be with you that is."

"Then it's settled," I said, addressing the bat and the whole congregation. "Please marry us now so we can leave immediately."

"What without a proper wedding reception?" gasped Luucy.

"You'd better at least do the honeymoon in here," Adeylia added, "while you still can."

"Fifty-year-olds in the real world can still honeymoon quite well," said Mary, giving her a sharp look.

"Well in here fifty-year-olds are dead," replied Adeylia.

It was getting on to dinnertime and Luucy was getting visibly nervous. So the bat married us using his shortest ceremony:

"Do you?" he said.

"We do," we said.

"Then it's done," he said.

"Are we married yet?" I asked.

"Aye lad, you're married. Now get her out of here before we get sentimental about how much we love her."

Mary did have tears in her eyes as we rushed out of Mousumerset Manor and fell down the third floor steps. We'd forgotten that fifty-year-olds can't glide down stairs like twelve-year-olds. But as we were picking each other up we noticed something that twelve-year-olds will never have. Not until they are fifty that is. We noticed five decades of splendor and experience fashioned into our faces by a Master Crafter. We noticed five decades of turning on the Master Potters wheel. We noticed five decades of refining by the Master Goldsmith.

And we noticed something else too, that we didn't have at twelve. Something that we could not acquire ourselves, or bestow on each other, or get from any human source. We noticed real manhood and true womanhood. This had ultimately and completely come from God our savior.

As we got to our feet He said, "Truly I say to you Mary, My child you are lovely in My sight. You are a woman. William, My child you have what it takes. You are a man."

And is it so surprising that a Master would turn out masterpieces? Mary was this indeed – the most radiant I had ever seen her. And her wide eyes told me she was seeing the same in me.

So with trembling arms we helped each other to our feet. Here at last was my Mary standing before me, all grown up and lovelier than ever. This was Mary, who had been trapped in her own bitterness, then captive by her own folly, but now embraced by her very own personal Lord and Master, Jesus Christ.

I placed my hand tenderly through her hair and around the back of her neck. Then we proceeded to prove that fifty-year-olds can indeed kiss. And believe me, the taste grows sweeter with age!

~32~
The Last Chapter

Yes, this is indeed the last chapter in The Dollhouse Trilogy. Thank you for hanging in there with me the whole way through. I hope you have learned something useful and I, for one, hope I have gained a new friend. You.

I'd like to tell you that Mary and I had lots of kids and lived happily ever after, but hey, this is the real world. The only kids we ever saw were Katherine's many grandchildren. They were great because we could give them back at the end of the day. All we had to do was feed them and prevent them from going up on the third floor. That and a few house repairs now and then.

Oh, I forgot to tell you that shortly after we were married Katherine came over to give me an urgent note which she had been carrying around in her purse. When she saw Mary standing beside me she burst out laughing and stuffed it back into her purse.

"What is it?" I pleaded, "give it to me."

"Oh, it's nothing anymore," she said, handing it over. "Here it is. Better late than never."

In elegant, tiny handwriting, the note said:

Willy, find me at Smary@ChâteauChic.com

We all had a hearty laugh about that.

As for James, we never heard from him again. But at night we could sometimes hear the faint sounds of swordfights and squeals of laughter coming from the third floor.

But hey, it was Mary and I who were living happily ever after. End of story.

Quotes quotable from <u>The Dollhouse Trilogy</u>:

from <u>Trapped</u>:

"Just being busy doesn't mean that our lives are rich and rewarding." Chapter 1

"Logic simply doesn't apply to dollhouses." Chapter 8.

"One word is worth a thousand pictures." The bat to Katherine in Chapter 13.

"Common courtesy is really so much more imperative than the deep quagmires of friendship – façade more important than fiber – masks more essential than morals." Luucy to girls in Chapter 15.

"Negative self image produces an inability to trust El." Luucy to girls in Chapter 15.

"If men became what we wanted, we wouldn't want them." Luucy to girls in Chapter 15.

"Prayers aren't magic words that can command doors to open for you." Katherine quoting the bat to the boys in Chapter 17.

"You don't have to believe it, for it to be true." Katherine to William in Chapter 17.

"Being correct to the letter is not superior to being right in principle, and being right is not better than being loving." The bat to William in Chapter 18.

"It's the beasts which turn out to be princes and the handsome princes which turn out to be beasts. Mary to William in Chapter 19 and in <u>Embraced</u> Chapter 14.

"Frogs are the birds of the lily pond and sliminess is meaningless under water. Their songs fill the night air." William to Mary in Chapter 19.

"Most humans remain forever trapped in fantasies of their own making." The bat to the children in Chapter 23.

"None of us should ever take ourselves too seriously." The bat to the children in Chapter 23.

"Magic *does work*, yet take heed of its evil source before you become consumed by it." The bat to the children in Chapter 23.

"In life everything is fully controlled by El and yet you are created with a faculty for independent action. This is a mystery that even bats can't fully fathom." The bat to the children in Chapter 23.

from <u>Captive</u>:

"Some ideas take a lot of pondering to sort out." Chapter 1.

"Fiction may be stranger than fact, but it's often more truthful." Chapter 1.

"Amalgamation of similar minds becomes the purest form of democracy, yet a most trivial form of society," Chapter 7.

"Snot rude, surprises sweet. You scum." Spider to Mary in Chapter 10.

"The foolish spiders call it the gusto way, but the wise call it the disgusto way." Chapter 10.

"To say it was dreamy might be to dream too much." On Mary's hair in Chapter 10.

"We often weave dangerous, sticky webs around our lives and then wonder why we get caught in them ourselves." Chapter 10.

"Courtesy is as courtesy does." Luucy to James in Chapter 12.

"The widow's walk, a sad result of misguided male courage and bravery." Chapter 12.

"You're probably just the little boy let out in you to chase off the man." Ivanhoho to James in Chapter 12.

"Ours are not just lives which pass through time, but rather it is time which, for a season passes through our lives." Ivanhoho to James in Chapter 12.

"Fantasy traps, while reality embraces." Ivanhoho to James in Chapter 12.

"Plain girls just get smacked down in their places, but pretty ones can twist everyone around them to their own ends."
Chapter 13.

"Beautiful creatures, bugs especially, will always climb up, while the uglier ones will always climb down." Chapter 13.

"Rescuers never knock, they simply bust the door down." Chapter 13.

"'Veni, vidi, vici!' loosely translated means, 'I'm here, see, so deal with it.' James in Chapter 13.

"It's the man that makes the clothes!" Mayrie to James in Chapter 13.

"La bottlle won't make you la man, land neither willll doilly-girll lupstairs." Marta to James in Chapter 14.

"What good is beauty enjoyed only by a mirror?" Mary in Chapter 15.

"You're in charge of us animals, although most humans seem to be sleeping on the job." Ivanhoho to Mary in Chapter 15.

"Bugs should know that their place is in the garden and not in houses!" Mary to Mayrie in Chapter 18.

"Limitation liz the sincerest form love fllattery," Marta in Chapter 19.

"Your mask doesn't make you into a superhero." Ivanhoho to Mary and James in Chapter 20.

"Contrition doesn't make up for a lack of proper upbringing." Luucy to Mary in Chapter 21.

"I'm already twelve, I don't need any more upbringing." Mary to Luucy in Chapter 21.

"Guys grow up frustratingly slow, and quite often never at all." Luucy to Mary in Chapter 21.

"Accomplishment is knowing how to do all the lady-like things, like cooking, eating, sewing, dressing, music, socializing and the like. Refinement is doing them without getting egg on your face." Luucy to Mary in Chapter 21.

"Violence is the last resort of the vanquished," Adeylia to Mary in Chapter 22.

"Ants always eat last, and only after everyone else has gone." Adeylia to James in Chapter 23.

"You can't tell a lass by her eyelashes." Sherwoode to James in Chapter 23.

"There are many doors to knowledge, but only one to wisdom, only one that leads to salvation." The bat to James in Chapter 25.

"Your own attitudes are all the magic you need to free yourself." The bat to James in Chapter 25.

from **Embraced**:

"You know your job is important when the company gives you lots of keys and a cell phone." Chapter 1

"Life is not a beauty pageant." Aunt Clara to Mary in Chapter 1

"All apples in fairy tales are poisonous." Mary in Chapter 1

"If you die to self – if you lose your life – then you will gain it." Marta quoting Ivanhoho to Mayrie in Chapter 4

"All real men have horses." Marta in Chapter 4

"Most men are bugs pretending to be people." Marta in Chapter 4

"It's not the weapons, but the man that handles them." The General in Chapter 6.

"Think of all the people who live with dogs and breathe their disgusting dog-breath day in and day out." Chapter 7

"In retirement years one just becomes busier than ever catching up on the real work that one was too busy to catch up on years ago." The Professor in Chapter 8.

"As a historian, aren't you just supposed to stick to the facts?" Mary to The Professor in Chapter 8.

"Nothing can deter determination." Chapter 9.

"You have to be lax before you can relax." Chapter 9.

"Growing up on the farm, they never gave names to animals they were going to eat." William in Chapter 15.

"Hair doesn't make a man." Mary to William in Chapter 15.

"Get hack beer!" Vick Cyrus to Mary in Chapter 15.

"There is always a cute little girl in horse movies." Chapter 16.

"Seeing through God's eyes is like putting on truth glasses which never fog up or lose focus." Chapter 16.

"It's never good to be overly or overtly in love with your looks." Mari to William in Chapter 19.

"Church rules only make you look good on the outside." Mari to William in Chapter 20.

"Sticks and stones may strike our heads but silly threats we never dreads." Spider to Mari in Chapter 22.

"Dreams are very self-centered things." Chapter 31.

"Is it so surprising that a Master would turn out masterpieces?" Chapter 31.

Codes:

Endnotes:

[1] Some of the events in chapter 26 are partially taken from the true story of Lieutenant Commander John McCain.

Matthew 5:4

You're blessed when you feel you've lost what is most dear to you. Only then can you be **embraced** by the One most dear to you.

The Holy Bible
The Message